They're Always With You

They're Always With You

Mary Clare Lockman

ISBN 13: 978-1-940014-97-5
eISBN 13: 978-1-940014-96-8
Library of Congress Number: 2013943635

Printed in the United States of America

17 16 15 14 13   5 4 3 2 1

Book Design by Mayfly Design
Typeset in Janson Text

Published by Wise Ink Creative Publishing
Minneapolis, Minnesota
www.wiseinkpub.com

To order contact **mclockman@msn.com**. Reseller discounts available.

To Ryan and Evan: May you always have a love of books.
You're the best. Love, Grandma

Acknowledgments

To all those who came to America in search of a better life for their families. Thank you. To Micky Martinson, RN, for telling me the story of her grandfather making and selling leather mittens during the Depression. And for letting me use it in my book. Thank you. To Marne McLevish for coming up with the perfect title. Thank you. To Connie Hill for reading my manuscript and giving me valuable feedback. Thank you. To Alison McGhee, teacher extraordinaire, for telling me there was a good story there waiting to come out. Thank you. To my family, as always, for your love and support. Thank you.

Chapter One

Who Is Daniel?

Secrets. Every family has them and mine is no exception.

They stay fiercely trapped within the walls of our house, as much a part of it as the plaster, wood, and nails. They're seen in the looks and eye contact which make the rounds to everyone in the room but me. They're found in the whispers late at night as I lay in bed trying to make sense of the jumbled words that float into my ears.

A name, Daniel, hovers in the air. The voices downstairs lower and soon there is silence. As the silence swells; it surrounds me. I pull the blanket around my arms and shoulders. The name Daniel lingers until its very presence hurts. I wrap the blanket even tighter. Who is Daniel thunders in my brain. I'll find out if it's the last thing I do.

Chapter Two

Colette

My name is Colette, Colette Antonia McGiver. I was born on October 12, 1958 in Red Wing, Minnesota, a town of about 10,000 people right on the Mississippi River.

I live with my parents, John and Gemma McGiver, my mom's sister, Aunt Florence, and my Grandfather, Antonio Rossini. I call him Gramps. He's my favorite, hands down. He calls me Bella; that's beautiful in Italian. One thing I know for sure is that I'm his favorite grandchild 'cause I'm the only one.

My family is small by anyone's standards but especially by my friends, who come from households of four to ten children. I've asked every kid in my sixth grade class at St. Anastasia if they have brothers and sisters. I've found to my horror that I'm the only person in the whole class of 58 kids who has no brothers or sisters.

My mom works in the office at my school. Since she has the same days off that I do, she loves her job. During summer vacation, my mom greets me every morning with the words, "My job is worth gold, pure gold." Then she does a little dance. Because, she says, all it takes is one person with some little ideas and then pretty soon there's trouble. When she puts it that way, I've accepted the fact that my mom will always be home with me.

Even though we both walk the seven blocks to school, my mom leaves before me in the morning. After school sometimes I'm home before her. I let myself in the back door since it's never locked. But usually she's waiting for me when I get home. She always asks me how my day at school was. I say, "Fine. And how was your day at school, Mom?"

I've also accepted the fact that whatever I do at school my mom will know about it. My teachers don't have to tell me that they'll be talking to my mom because I know teachers talk all the time. And their favorite subjects are their students and the student's families.

Saturday mornings I eat breakfast with Mom, Dad, and Gramps. Aunt Florence works as a nurse in the hospital so she works lots of weekends and holidays. She doesn't seem to mind the weekends 'cause she never goes out at night anyway. And I don't mind her working weekends and holidays because then I don't have to hear her tsk, tsk as she looks at me like I'm not doing enough to help my mom. I want to say, "Aunt Florence, I'm only one kid and I can't do everything! Why don't you help more?" But if I said that my mom would be mad because for some strange reason she's very protective of Aunt Florence. So I don't say anything but it bugs me no end.

This morning I was alone with my mom. Dad and Gramps were shopping in the lumberyard. They're going to build a new garage in place of the old tumbling down one behind the house. Anyway, I decided to ask my mom some questions during breakfast since there was no one to interrupt us.

"Did Aunt Florence ever have a boyfriend?" I watched every movement of my mom's face.

"Yes, she had a boyfriend years ago." My mom spooned the scrambled eggs onto my plate. "Enough?" she asked with the spoon poised in the air.

"Yeah, that's enough. What was his name?"

"I don't remember." My mom returned the pan to the stove and now was holding another pan. "Bacon?"

"Sure." Two pieces of bacon landed on my plate. I moved them away from my eggs.

"Eat, Colette. Your eggs will get cold."

"Was it Clarence, Frederic, or maybe Daniel?" I snuck in Daniel at the end so I could watch my mom's reaction. I was careful not to emphasize Daniel any more than the others.

"It wasn't any of those but I really don't remember his name."

I didn't believe it for a second. My mom remembered everything. She could tell me stories from her childhood that made me feel I was right there with her. She knew the names of all her grade school friends, every member in their families, and even the name of their family dogs. Sometimes I would quiz her just to see if she really remembered or if she was making it up. She passed my quizzes with flying colors. No problem.

"Was Aunt Florence in love?" I took a bite of bacon, chewing first on one side of my mouth and then the other.

"With whom?"

"With her boyfriend. You know, the one whose name you can't remember."

My mom sat across the table from me. She looked up from her plate of eggs and bacon. "Yes, I think she was in love. Why do you ask?"

"Because I just can't picture Aunt Florence in love. She never even smiles."

"Florence was always a little serious."

"A little?"

"Being serious isn't such a bad thing. She works hard and she's dependable. Why are you giving me the third degree about Florence?"

"I'm interested, that's all. I wonder why sometimes she stares at me without saying anything." Aunt Florence had glared at me in her irritating way last night. I asked her if something was wrong. She said no, like she always did. And then she tightened her lips until they almost disappeared. I wanted to yell, "Then why are you staring at me?" But I just bit my bottom lip instead.

"Florence has had kind of a sad life. Be nice."

"I am nice. I don't say half the things I think. In fact, I've thought about asking her if she could just smile once in a while. Would that hurt her?"

"I'm glad you didn't say that."

"Don't worry. I won't say it." I bit into my last forkful of eggs. "Why was Aunt Florence's life so sad?"

"A lot of things happen in people's lives and some are really sad. You'll find that out when you get older."

My mom always talked about what I would find out and understand when I got older. I was getting older all the time, eleven and a half next month, and I could understand some of these things if she would just tell them to me. "Did her boyfriend, Daniel, leave her or something?"

"She didn't have a boyfriend named Daniel."

"I thought you didn't remember his name."

"I remember it wasn't Daniel."

I wanted to tell my mom that I'd heard them talking last night about Daniel but I decided not to. I had mentioned the name Daniel twice in the conversation and she hadn't reacted. Instead I asked a question that I asked about every two months. It usually got a rise out of her. "When is Aunt Florence going to find her own place?"

"Colette, I thought you were going to be nice. What happened?" My mom cleared the plates off the table. "Are you done?"

My mom was done with more than breakfast so there was no point in asking more questions. "Anyway, I'm glad you're my mom instead of Aunt Florence."

"I'm glad you're my kid too. Now I have a question. Did your teacher mention the movie, "Becoming a Woman?""

I moved around in my chair. "Mrs. Bosworth said something about it."

"What did she say?"

My mom loved talking to all the teachers at school. She said it was a little extra benefit of her job. "I'm sure you talked to her. What'd she say to you?"

"Well, she said we're supposed to go to school together on Monday night. They'll show the movie to the sixth grade girls with their mothers."

"Wonderful. Maybe we can skip it."

"You can't skip it, Colette. Mrs. Bosworth said this is an experiment this year. They've always shown it to the eighth graders."

"Believe me, I can wait till eighth grade."

"You're really funny. Do you have any questions before we see the movie?"

"No. I really don't." I pushed my chair back.

"I've been meaning to talk to you about, well, about puberty." She held her hands together in front of her apron.

"Mom. Stop." I covered my ears. I stood up.

"Okay. I know it's embarrassing so I'll stop. One more question though. What are you doing today?"

"Playing basketball at the gym. Some of my friends will be there and I might go over to Sally's later."

"Please straighten your room first. Call me when you get to Sally's." My mom took the glasses and silverware from the table and brought them to the sink.

"Clean it right now?"

She bent down to get the dishpan and the dish soap from underneath the sink. "Right now."

Arguing with my mom made her really stubborn and then she wouldn't budge in anything. I didn't like giving up so easily but I couldn't wait to talk to my best friend, Sally, about Aunt Florence being in love.

I went upstairs to my bedroom. I loved my room because I had gotten my own record player for Christmas. I still couldn't believe it. The record player sat on a wooden stand that had a shelf underneath for the records. I kept it away from the window because I couldn't take the chance that our sometimes blustery weather would blow one of my Beatles records onto the floor. If any of them got scratched or broken, I'd probably scream at the top of my lungs. Then I'd sit on the floor and cry.

I always put a record carefully on the turntable and watched to make sure the needle didn't skip. Then I turned up the music really loud and sang along. I knew all the Beatle's songs. Every single word. My happy reverie usually resulted in a pounding at my door and my mom yelling, "Will you turn it down so the rest of us can think!" I wanted to say, "Why did you get me a record player if I can't even listen to my records?" But instead, I just mumbled under my breath and then turned down the music.

I needed music for cleaning so I grabbed an album as soon as I walked into my room. I turned on the record player and pretty soon I was singing away. In less than 30 minutes I picked my clothes up off the floor, put them in the hamper in the bathroom, swept my cold wooden floor, made my bed, and dusted my dresser. Then I raced down the steps and yanked my spring jacket off the hanger in the closet.

"Bye, Mom." I yelled as I ran out the back door.

Chapter Three

One-on-One

I sprinted down the back steps. Even though it was early March, most of the snow had melted except for stubborn icy patches in the shadows of our evergreens. I breathed in the crisp newness in the air.

My bike waited in our tumbling down garage. I rolled it away from its spot leaning against the wall. Soon I was out in the sunshine pedaling the eight blocks to the gym.

I was ecstatic this year because I actually made the Varsity team. I practiced every day after school for an hour and a half. That was required of everyone so Saturday practice was optional. I liked Saturdays the best because boys were there from the boy's basketball team. They played hard and they weren't afraid to grab the ball away from me so I've learned to be quick. Since I'm only four foot eleven, my quickness has given me a little edge. Anyway, I had to practice every chance I could because the 1970 City Championship game was only ten days away.

I walked into the gym. I waved to Shannon Doyle and Kate Gustafson. They were eighth graders on my team and starters for every game. I heard my name above the clatter of basketballs being dribbled and bounced.

"Hey, Colette, how about some one-on-one," Bobby Bennett said. Bobby was a sixth grader who was on the boy's team.

"Sure, I'm ready." Who gets the ball first?"

"You got it last time."

"Okay. Up to ten."

"Okay." Bobby bent down at the waist and started dribbling as he looked into my eyes. He switched the ball from hand to hand and then shifted suddenly to the right. I moved with him and kept flicking my hand toward the ball. He smirked a little, stopped, and did a jump shot. Swish. The ball sailed through the net. "Try to beat that," he said.

"No problem."

Rules for girls were different than for boys. The girls could only dribble three times and then we had to pass the ball. Since I was a pretty good dribbler, it bugged me no end. It was hard to set up strategy when you had to stop and pass, stop and pass. Each team had three guards on one side and three forwards on the other so we could only go as far as the center line. The coaches said it kept anyone from being a ball hog.

If they'd asked me, I would have said there were plenty of ball hogs to go around. Like Patty Bloomer, for instance. She got the ball, took her three dribbles, and then she'd shoot this wild shot from wherever she happened to be. The other team usually didn't even guard her. They just let her shoot the ball nowhere near the basket and then we all scrambled for it. Luckily, she didn't play very often. Even though she was in eighth grade and it was her last year on the team, the coach only put her in when we were way ahead. The bad thing was she came in when the sixth graders did so I had to play with her. I would dribble three times and then look around for the other forward who had two guards surrounding her. I ended up passing to the Bloomer, as we called her, and then raced lickety-split for the basket. Then I planted myself right by the basket and waited for the air ball that was sure to come.

The rumor was that the rules were changing next year. In the meantime, it wasn't hard to understand why I loved Saturday practice. I could dribble a hundred times if I wanted to before I took a shot.

I grabbed the ball from Bobby and got ready. I held the ball with both my hands and moved to the left. As quickly as I did that, I changed direction and went to the right. Bobby couldn't keep up with me so it was an easy score. I put the ball into the box on the backboard and it went right in. I didn't need to say anything; my raised eyebrows and smile did the job.

We were neck and neck up to nine. Nine to nine and you had to win by one.

Bobby tried a fake but I was ready for him. I batted the ball away and we both went after it. I got to it before it went out of bounds and pivoted around.

I'd been watching the Harlem Globetrotters on television so I liked to dribble really low to the ground. Bobby didn't try to get the ball; he just waited patiently for me to either shoot or drive towards the basket. I felt pretty confident that I was going to beat him so I decided to get it over with. I stopped dribbling, set my feet, and Bobby was all over me. His arms were waving in all directions. "Foul," I yelled. "You can't do that."

"Who said? Go ahead and shoot." Bobby continued moving his arms wildly.

"You're cheating." I couldn't dribble any more because I had stopped and I couldn't shoot either. "You don't win if you cheat."

"Okay, I'll let you shoot." Bobby hung back a little. "But I'm not admitting that I'm cheating."

I knew this was my only chance. I arced the ball toward the basket. Bobby leaped towards the ball and blocked it mid-air. He dashed behind the free throw line, dribbling all the way, set, and did a jump shot. I couldn't stop it. Swish. It went through the basket without touching the rim.

I stood there for a minute while Bobby whooped and laughed. Then I remembered I had to go over to Sally's to talk about Aunt Florence. "I still say you cheated but I gotta go," I said.

"Two out of three?"

"Nope, I'm going to Sally's."

"Next week?"

"Sure," I said. "I'll see you later."

I rode my bike the five blocks over to Sally's. I heard the noise in her house while I stood on the porch waiting for someone to answer the bell. Sally had an older brother, John, who was two years older than her, and four younger brothers and sisters. I liked the noise in her house most of the time. Sally said my house was heaven because it was so quiet and there were no little brothers and sisters wrecking my things or bursting in on me when I changed clothes.

"C'mon in, Colette." Sally opened the door.

Two of Sally's brothers chased each other through the living room while making popping sounds. Four-year-old Eric waved to me as he raced by. I waved to him. His seven-year-old brother Joe pointed his finger at Eric pretending to shoot him. Eric stopped, clasped his chest, and fell over.

"Ignore them. They're annoying," Sally said. "Let's go to my room."

"I've got to call home first."

"You know where the phone is."

Underneath the stairway was a cool loveseat with a small, rectangular table next to it. The phone sat on the table. I liked sitting on the loveseat while I called home.

Sally shared her room with Anna and Margaret, her little sisters. Two double beds positioned themselves on opposite ends of the room parallel to each other. Since Sally was older than Anna by almost two years, she got one of the double beds to herself. It bugged Anna no end so she made comments every time I saw her like, "Do you think it's fair?" I always pretended I didn't know what she was talking about so I'd say things like, "What's fair?" Then Anna would say, "You know." I'd say, "No. I don't know." It was kind of fun at this point because while Sally rolled her eyes, Anna shifted back and forth on her feet because she didn't want to appear jealous. "Well," she'd say, "When am I going to have a bed to myself?" Sally always interrupted with, "Leave us. Get out."

We looked around the room, even in the closet, to make sure no one hid behind the hanging clothes. We both plopped on Sally's bed and lay there facing each other.

"Okay, give, what'd your mom say?" Sally rearranged her pillow and propped her head up with her hand.

"I'll tell you in a minute. First, are you going to school Monday night with your mom?"

"My mom said I have to," Sally said. "Yuck."

"Did she tell you the name of the movie?"

"Becoming a Woman."

"At least the boys won't be with us because they'll be in their own room watching a movie with the dads."

"I wonder if their movie is called "Becoming a Maaan." Sally giggled.

It sounded so funny the way she stretched out man that I laughed until I had tears coming down my cheeks. I said, "Just wait until I become a womaaan."

Now Sally had tears coming down her cheeks. She grabbed some tissues and handed me a couple. She blew her nose hard. "We'll talk about it more after the big event." She blew her nose again.

"Agreed." I blew my nose. "Let's make sure that we sit together."

"Agreed. Now tell me what your mom said about your aunt."

"Mom said she knew for a fact that Aunt Florence had been in love." I wiped the tears off both my cheeks.

"Really?"

"Really."

"Who was she in love with?"

"I don't know," I said. "But the point is, can you picture Aunt Florence being in love?"

"It's hard to picture, that's for sure."

"You think she ever kissed him?"

"Of course she did," Sally said. "You said she was in love."

"I suppose you're right. How do you picture him?"

"I think he was probably really, really cute and he swept your aunt right off her feet." With her free hand, Sally made a large sweeping motion.

"You think she smiled when she was with him?"

"All the time. She kissed him, didn't she?"

"Yes, she sure did." I was now convinced that Aunt Florence had been in love and that kissing was a big part of it. "You know what else, Sal? They were talking about Daniel again last night. I heard his

18

name, some other words, and then there was silence. Complete silence."

"Did you ask your mom about it?"

"I tried but she didn't react when I mentioned his name." I told Sally about the entire conversation with my mom in the morning.

"That is so weird."

"I know. I even asked my mom if Daniel was Aunt Florence's boyfriend."

"Maybe. Maybe he was."

"She said he wasn't."

"Maybe she's lying."

"No, she wouldn't lie to me. Sometimes, she doesn't answer or she changes the subject but what she tells me is the truth."

"Who is he, then?"

We heard a timid knock on the door. Since I knew who it was, and since I loved her best of all Sally's family except for Sally, I went to open the door. Five-year-old Margaret stood twirling her thick, blond hair around her chubby fingers. I opened my arms wide. Margaret leapt into my arms and I held her up in the air. I brought her into the room and dropped her onto Sally's bed.

"Can I talk too?" Margaret asked.

"What do you want to talk about?" Sally asked.

"What you guys are talking about."

"That's for big girls. Let's talk about kindergarten." Sally tickled her sister's feet for just a second.

"I'm big too." Margaret sat up straighter on the bed and puffed out her chest.

"I've got to go. It's ten to five." I started moving towards the door.

"Oh, d'you have to?" Margaret sounded so disappointed that I stopped walking and came back to the bed.

"How would you like it if next time I come over, you're in the room with us and we can talk the whole time?" I hugged her again.

"Okay. Promise?"

"I promise. But right now I have to go."

Chapter Four

An Invitation

At dinner that night I couldn't take my eyes off Aunt Florence. I kept trying not to stare but I couldn't help it. I tried and tried to picture her madly in love; smiling away. Suddenly Aunt Florence was more than interesting; she was fascinating. I looked up from my plate. As soon as she looked at me, I looked back down but somehow my plate was nowhere near as interesting as Aunt Florence.

Each morning before going to the hospital, Aunt Florence pulled her thick, reddish-brown hair away from her face and pinned it up in the back. I had the same wavy, reddish-brown hair as Aunt Florence. I did wear a ponytail sometimes but I knew I would never want to pull my hair into a tight, pin-filled bun. It drew her skin tight against her cheekbones and made them kind of stick out. The other thing the daily ritual of hair pulling up accomplished for Aunt Florence was it gave her the perfect place to put her starched nursing hat. She spent a lot of time getting that hat on just right in the morning. When she got home, she carefully put it on her dresser in a little space off to the side.

Now that I looked, really looked at Aunt Florence, I noticed her golden-colored skin was flawless. There wasn't a wrinkle or a mole or a pimple or even a freckle. I couldn't believe I hadn't noticed before this moment how perfect Aunt Florence's skin was.

Something else I hadn't noticed before was that Aunt Florence's eyes were a very unusual color; almost the color of my favorite blue jeans. I could barely see her denim blue eyes through those drab, overly large brown glasses. If she had different glasses…

"Colette," my dad said. "Hello."

"Hi, Dad." I smiled. My dad was one of the coolest people in the world. He could do anything and I mean anything.

"You're usually talking our ears off. You haven't said one word since we sat down. You okay?"

"Of course, I'm okay. I'm just letting others talk." I don't know if it was because I was the one and only but my dad asked me if I was okay at least once a week. He said that he hoped I would tell him if something was bothering me. I always told him that of course I would tell him but it was hard when what

22

was bothering me was nothing at school or in the neighborhood. It was the secret somebody in the house named Daniel.

"How was basketball?" my dad asked. His index finger tapped against his lips.

"Fine."

"Are you ready for the big game next week?"

"I think so."

"Good. Want to see what Gramps and I got at the lumberyard today?"

"Sure, Dad, I'd love to."

"After dinner, okay?"

"Okay." Nothing interested me more than being part of my dad's projects. He had lots of special tools, all different kinds of saws, and every size of screwdriver. Sometimes he let me use the screwdrivers or a hammer and nails but he would never let me try any of his saws. He said they were too dangerous.

He had finished the basement several years ago so Aunt Florence could have a bedroom, bathroom, and sitting room all to herself. Sometimes I went down in the basement to the laundry room and, if Aunt Florence's door was open, I snuck a look and there I saw her nursing hat resting in its spot on the dresser.

Last winter, my dad made new kitchen cabinets with the help of Gramps and me. Gramps supplied the muscle, my dad said, while I supplied the entertainment. We talked as I handed my dad and Gramps their special tools. Sometimes Gramps talked about growing up on a farm in Italy. He had lived there with his parents and his sister, Sofia. Other times Gramps talked about taking a ship from Naples, Italy to New York City. That led to stories about seeing the Statue of Liberty for the first time and going through Ellis Island.

I loved it when Gramps talked about how he ended up in Red Wing, Minnesota. He had bought a pharmacy with a soda fountain during the early thirties. The store's been part of our family ever since. My dad worked there on Saturdays when he was in high school. Since my mom worked there in high school too, pretty soon one thing led to another and they started going out. And the rest is history, as my mom would say.

At some point Gramps convinced my dad to go to pharmacy school so he could buy into the business and become Gramp's partner. They worked together as partners until last summer when Gramps retired. Now my dad's the only owner.

Anyway, I hoped Gramps would be in a talking mood while we built the new garage.

I had to do dishes before I could go out to the garage. That was my daily job except for Sundays.

Four other people lived in the house but it was my job to do the dishes. I heard their reasons loud and clear. Mom cooked the meal. Dad worked all day. Aunt Florence worked all day. Gramps, well, he was Gramps. So that's the way it was in our house. About once a week, I argued about the unfairness of it. My dad wouldn't say anything but my mom would set her feet flat on the floor, put her hands on her hips, jut out her chin, and go into her I'm not going to budge mode. If I kept arguing, the only thing that happened was that I had to scrub the pans too.

I started the dishes immediately, before the table was even cleared. I had to fill the dishpan with dish soap, put the plates in the pan, rub them front and back with the sponge, rinse them with warm, never cold water, and then line them up in the rack to dry. Of course, there wasn't enough room for all the dishes in the rack so I'd have to dry some of the plates to have room for cups and glasses. My mom put the dishes back in the cupboard.

I thought sometime soon we should get a dishwasher. Some of my friends had dishwashers in their kitchens. Take Sally's family, for instance. They had this large dishwasher in the kitchen that had to be hooked up to the hot and cold water every time it washed. It took up the whole middle of the kitchen

and it shook and shuddered while it washed. Sometimes the water sprayed all over the kitchen. Then
the younger kids ran around and screamed and Mrs.
Reynolds yelled at Mr. Reynolds that he hadn't tightened the connections tight enough. It was really
funny. When the dishes were done, the whole thing
was disconnected and stored next to the sink. Mrs.
Reynolds said she couldn't live without it.

I knew if I had one I'd feel exactly the same way as
Mrs. Reynolds. Every time I told my mom what Mrs.
Reynolds said, she answered, "The Reynoldses have
eight people living in their house. They should have
a dishwasher." We had five people, more than half
of what Sally's family had so I didn't know why we
couldn't have a small dishwasher. I decided right then
and there that when I grew up I was going to have a
large dishwasher so none of my children had to wash
dishes by hand.

"Colette, go with your dad. I'll finish," my mom
said. She tied her apron around her waist and started
putting on the yellow rubber gloves she used for
doing the dishes.

I couldn't believe my ears but I didn't wait around
for her to change her mind. I wiped my wet hands on
the towel hanging under the sink and yelled for my
dad. "Dad, I'm ready."

The garage hadn't been used for my dad's car for a while since the one side hadn't been straight for as long as I could remember. My dad said he didn't want it to fall down with his car in it. Aunt Florence said she felt the same way so she always parked her car in front of our house, rain or shine.

My dad opened the door to the garage. I walked in first. "Wow," I said.

Different sizes and lengths of boards filled one whole side of the garage. They were stacked one on top of another.

"When are you going to start?" I asked.

"Sometime in May. It'll depend on the weather. We have to knock down the old garage first. That will probably take two or three days. Then we can start framing the new garage."

My dad said he counted pills all day so when he got a chance to work with his hands he took advantage of it. Those were his exact words.

"I'll get my hammer and nails ready." The garage would be my dad's biggest project yet and I planned on being there all the way. I could have asked my dad more about his plans for the garage but I had Aunt Florence on my mind, big time. "Do you like Aunt Florence?"

"I like Florence. Why do you ask?"

"I was just wondering if you liked her, with her never smiling and all."

"Yes, I do like her. Let's go back to the house."

I knew this was my chance since there was always someone else around listening. I decided to just blurt it out. "Mom said she was in love when she was young and that she had a boyfriend."

"Oh, that's what this is all about."

"Well."

"Well what?"

"Was she in love?"

"Yes, Florence was in love. Isn't that what Mom told you?"

"Yeah. I just wanted to see if you thought so too."

"C'mon, let's go." My dad opened the garage door and guided me out in front of him.

"You know what, Dad?" I had planned on bringing up the hush-hush Daniel when I was alone with my dad, but this didn't seem like the right time since we were talking about Aunt Florence. "I think I'm going to ask Aunt Florence if she wants to come to my basketball game."

"I bet she'd like that. Your mom said that Florence was a very good basketball player." He closed the garage door.

I stopped right where I was walking. I couldn't believe it. "She used to play?"

"Yes, she played basketball."

This was too much. Aunt Florence had never shown any interest in my games. How many other things didn't I know about my one and only aunt on my mom's side?

"Do you think she'll come to the game?"

"I don't know. Ask her."

"Will she think it's weird since we never talk?"

"I don't know, honey. You won't know unless you ask her."

Aunt Florence sat in the living room reading a book. Gramps and my mom were there too. I decided to just blurt out my question in front of everyone because there was less chance of her turning me down if everyone was staring at her.

"Aunt Florence?"

"What?" She looked up from her book.

"Would you like to come to my city championship game a week from Tuesday?" I stood first on one foot and then the other and the room seemed smaller than it had before. I felt my heart beat out its rhythm. I was sure my dad could hear it pounding too. He stood a little behind me.

"I may be working," Aunt Florence said.

"Oh, that's okay." I looked down at the floor.

"I'll check my schedule."

"If you can't go, it's okay."

"I'll try. I really will. Colette?"

"What?" I turned.

"Thanks. I used to love basketball."

The weirdest thing happened right then, right in the middle of our living room. Aunt Florence smiled at me and I smiled back. It seemed like a perfectly natural thing to do.

Chapter Five

Sundays

The next day was Sunday and we all went to church like we did every week. My mom woke me about 8:15 am to get ready for 9:00 o'clock Mass. Supposedly, Sunday was a day of rest but I sure wasn't allowed to. I reminded my mom of that about twice a month but she always shrugged her shoulders and said, "You can rest when we get home."

We had to get dressed up for church. My dad wore a suit with a tie. Gramps added a vest to his suit and tie and topped the whole thing off with one of his many hats. And his shoes were so shiny that I could see my face in them. My mom said he looked very dapper. My mom wore a dress no matter what the weather was. It could be 20 below zero and she still wore a dress. I had begged and begged for years not to have to wear a dress to church. My mom finally said I could wear pants as long as they weren't jeans. I didn't argue, believe me.

Personally, I thought Mass was overrated. Everyone filed in, blessed themselves with the holy water, knelt on one knee, and then slid into a pew. Talking wasn't allowed. We sat there not talking and waited for the priest, Father Walsh. Once he arrived, everyone stood up. Then we spent the next hour standing, kneeling, sitting, standing, kneeling, sitting while we listened to readings and terrible high-pitched singing voices from the choir.

Mrs. O'Neill was the absolute worst of all the ladies. She took a song to new heights, as my dad would say. Although people tried, it was impossible to sing along with Mrs. O'Neill and the rest of the ladies. Sometimes it all blended together, but other times I actually covered my ears, it was so awful. When I did that either my mom or dad looked at me until I took my hands away from my ears.

Gramps sang every note of every song. He could carry a tune and, believe me, he was better than the ladies in the choir.

"Gramps, you really should try out for lead singer of the choir," I said just about every week. "Your voice could drown out Mrs. O'Neill's and maybe she'd give up singing forever."

Gramps said with a laugh, "Don't you know that Italians love opera. You should too."

"If that's opera, I'll just have to pass."

Certain songs made Gramps cry. I'd hear him sniffling and then I'd sneak a peek at him and he'd be wiping his eyes. Sometimes, I just put my arm around Gramps and we stood together while he sniffled and wiped his eyes.

"Are you thinking about Italy and all the family you left," I asked him once.

"No, Bella," he said, "I'm thinking about your Grandmother Rose."

I didn't like Gramp's nickname for me because I couldn't picture a "Bella" girl playing basketball. She'd probably play with dolls and I didn't like dolls. Not at all. Anyway, I was just going to ask another question when I heard Gramps say, "Shh. Pay attention." He bent down and put his finger to his mouth.

This Sunday, the Mass and even Father Walsh's sermon flew by because I was trying to picture Aunt Florence playing basketball. It was still pretty difficult. I wondered if Aunt Florence had ever played one-on-one. Or if she knew how to shoot a jump shot.

As we walked out of the church, I saw Sally and her family. The eight of them went to church every Sunday. I enjoyed sitting behind them because Sally's two little brothers, Eric and Joe, poked each other and made faces from the time people started saying "Lord

Have Mercy." It was only about five minutes into the Mass and by the time people were singing the "Gloria" it was full-fledged warfare in the Reynolds family. Eric and Joe were then moved to the outside with one parent beside each of them. Even with that the boys wiggled and wriggled until they caught sight of each other. As soon as they did their tongues pointed at each other and the parents pulled each of the boys towards them while whispering into their ears.

Gramps was too intent on his responses to the priest to even notice but my mom always looked at my dad and kind of smiled. If Aunt Florence was there she tsked, tsked very quickly, one tsk running into the next until I couldn't figure out how many tsks she was actually making. I had to cover my mouth to keep from laughing.

My mom would say those two boys were surely a handful and that she admired women like Mrs. Reynolds who could raise so many kids and keep their sanity. Then she'd look at me and say it was times like this that made her really appreciate her one child. I would say, "Well, Mom, it's never too late to change that."

"Sal, what are you doing later?" Sally and I stood in the back of church while our parents talked. Mrs. Reynolds shook her head back and forth while looking at her two boys. My mom listened intently and then shook her head back and forth in sympathy for Mrs. Reynolds.

"We have family coming over for Anna's birthday," Sally said. "I'll call you after they leave."

Gramps liked going out to breakfast on Sundays. We usually went to a little neighborhood diner and Gramps had bacon, eggs over hard, and hash browns. I always had pancakes.

"How're your pancakes, Colette?" Gramps asked. He asked me the same question every single time we went out to breakfast.

"Fine. How're your eggs, Gramps?" I asked him the same question every time we went out to breakfast.

"They're great, just the way I like them." Gramps had a forkful of hashbrowns just waiting near his mouth. He placed the forkful inside his mouth and said, "Mmm." Then he chewed with a happy look on his face. My mom said that she had never seen a person who enjoyed meals more than Gramps. She was right. He raved every night about my mom's meals.

"I'm shocked that you like them." I said. "In fact, it's a real surprise." Gramps stopped eating long enough to make eye contact with my dark, where-are-the-pupil eyes. He didn't have to smile. His dark, where-are-the-pupil eyes did it for him.

"When is your big game?" my dad asked.

"In nine days. We're playing St. Margaret and they're really, really good."

"Are you ready?"

"I think so. I probably won't even play and if I do I'll have the wonderful misfortune of having to pass to the Bloomer so she can shoot like a crazy person. Sometimes I wave my arms and yell to let her know I'm open and she still shoots it."

"Maybe she doesn't see you," my mom said. "What I mean is, maybe she needs glasses."

"I never thought of that." I took a bite of my pancake and thought about it. Maybe the Bloomer really couldn't see. "You may be right, Mom. The Bloomer might be blind as a bat. That would explain her never shooting or passing anywhere near the basket."

"Do you still want to interview me for school?" Gramps asked. "How about this afternoon?"

"Okay. That would be great."

On Friday, my teacher, Mrs. Bosworth, had hung a world map in front of my class. She asked each of us to put a tack in the country where our ancestors came from. I put a tack in Italy for Gramps and Ireland for my other grandparents. Some of the kids put tacks in four different countries."

Anyway, we were supposed to find out as much as we could about our ancestors. Why they left their countries and then what they did once they came to America. She said to go to the library to find out about each country. I was so happy because I had Gramps living right in my house.

"Should we meet in the sunroom, Colette?" Gramps asked as we drove home.

"Sure."

"One o'clock. I'll see you there."

Chapter Six

Gramps leaves Italy

Our house wasn't huge or anything but I loved it. It had a small sunroom off the kitchen that caught every ray of sunlight. I loved to sit in the big stuffed armchair while stripes of sun came through the windows and landed on me, warming me from the outside in. My mom loved to curl up in the loveseat with a book. There was a writing desk in the corner that my dad used for drawing his building projects and for paying bills. Gramps said the room was well-used.

At exactly one o'clock, I walked into the sunroom with a notebook. Gramps was waiting for me.

"Do you want the chair?"

"No. I'll take the loveseat." I opened my notebook and looked at the questions I had written down. "First of all, if there's anything you don't want to answer, don't feel like you have to." Even though Gramps had talked about Italy and Ellis Island before and I had asked him lots of questions, this seemed different.

"Fire away." Gramps sat down in the big armchair.

I cleared my throat. "Well, Gramps, why did you come here?"

"I grew up on a farm with my parents and my sister, Sofia. We didn't own the land so my Papa was always worried about money and taking care of us. I saw nothing in my future but working the farm and barely surviving." Gramps ran his hand through his hair. "And I wanted to see what America was all about."

"What had you heard about America?"

"That you could work and make money. That appealed to me."

"What year was it?"

"1923."

"How old were you?

"19."

"Were your parents upset?"

"My Papa was very angry. He asked me who was going to help him work the farm over and over. My mother wouldn't come to Naples to see me off because she said her heart was broken enough."

"Was it hard to say good-bye?"

"Very hard. I can still see my mother crying." Gramps dabbed his eyes with a tissue he was holding. He cleared his throat.

I hoped Gramps didn't cry because I never knew what to say if someone started crying. I looked at my notebook again. "Who took you to Naples?"

"Papa and Sofia took me. We had a donkey and a cart so it took almost half a day to get to Naples. Papa and Sofia dropped me off at a dorm and then they turned around and went home." Gramps ran his fingers through his snow-white hair.

I was writing as fast as I could. I didn't want to miss a word. "What was the dorm for?"

"The ships demanded that we stay in a dorm for two weeks. They only wanted to transport healthy people so my head was shaved for lice and I had a full medical exam."

I tried to picture myself all alone without my family. And then going to a brand new country. I couldn't do it. "Was it scary in the dorm?"

"It was a little scary. But I was young so I only thought about the possibilities. And I met a boy my age named Giovanni. We were together in the dorm and on the ship. That helped a lot. We talked and talked about what we were going to do in America. He was going to live with his Uncle Geno in New York and I was going to live with Papa's cousin, Beto, in Chicago."

"When did you get to New York City?"

"Our ship arrived in New York City on June 7,

1923. I stood with Giovanni as we pulled into the harbor and saw the Statue of Liberty. People on the ship were waving and crying and everyone was smiling. Giovanni slapped my back and said, 'I can't believe we're here. I can't believe we're here.'"

"I bet the Statue of Liberty is really cool."

"She's cool all right. She was a beautiful sight."

"Was Ellis Island there too?"

"Yes, it's close to where the Statue of Liberty is. Giovanni and I walked into the huge, main room in Ellis Island and saw lots and lots of people standing in lines. There was so much noise that I couldn't understand anything anyone was saying. We moved along slowly until we met the first inspector. He waved us upstairs." Gramps stood up. He liked to use his hands when he talked. "There another inspector had a piece of chalk he used to mark people. A woman who was limping was marked with an L, a man who held onto his lower belly was marked with an H, another man who seemed confused by all the commotion was marked with an X." His fingers drew each of the letters in the air. "I guess they went into different lines."

"So what did you do upstairs?"

"We had to read in Italian and put wooden blocks in the right sized holes. We had to stand still while an inspector with a buttonhook pulled our eyelids down."

"What for?"

"They were looking for an eye disease called trachoma. The disease was very, very contagious. If you showed any evidence of it, the inspectors might send you right back where you came from."

"So they would have sent you back to Italy?"

"Yes."

"Was that the last inspector?"

"No. One more inspector asked me if I had a job. He also wanted to know if I had a place to stay and enough money to get there."

"Did you?"

"Giovanni had convinced me to come with him and work in his uncle's tile factory. And I had $5.20."

"Oh, Gramps." I stopped writing in my notebook.

"Five dollars was a lot of money in 1923. I was happy I had that much. They wanted you to have a little more but I told them I had a place to stay."

"Did the inspector say anything else?"

"He compared my name with the ship list and then wrote it down. He said, 'Good luck. Welcome to America.'"

"How long did it take you to get through Ellis Island?"

"About four hours."

"Then where did you go?"

"We took a ferryboat across the bay. Giovanni's Uncle Geno was waiting for us. Giovanni introduced me to his uncle and then asked if I could work in the factory. Uncle Geno said he had a place for me too."

"Did you stay with them?"

"Yes. And Giovanni and I went to work at the tile factory. We loaded and unloaded trucks."

"How long did you work there?"

"For just three weeks."

"How come?"

"Giovanni was in a terrible accident. He was crushed by a truck that was backing up. The driver didn't see him. He died before the ambulance came." Gramps stopped talking.

"How sad."

"It was terrible. Uncle Geno was beside himself. He didn't know how he was going to tell his sister in Italy. So I left. I wanted to get to Chicago as soon as possible."

"That must have been hard for you, Gramps."

"It was very difficult. Giovanni was so young and full of life. He had so many dreams. He will always be with me." Gramps put his hand over his heart.

My throat felt kind of tight, almost like one of those huge boa constrictors was squeezing it. I didn't want Gramps to see my eyes brimming with tears so I cleared my throat and blinked my eyelids hard. I was afraid he wouldn't tell me any more of his stories if he thought he was making me feel bad. And he'd be right because I felt so bad for Gramps right then.

"Did you ever see your parents again?" I asked.

"Never. I didn't have the money to begin with, then the Depression hit and World War Two happened."

"Plus, you met Grandma Rose."

"And that's a whole different story."

He seemed kind of tired after all the talk about leaving Italy, going through Ellis Island, and especially Giovanni. I looked in my notebook. On the last page was the question, WHO IS DANIEL? I had underlined it twice and circled it. I covered it with my hand before Gramps saw the question. "I guess we're finished, Gramps. Thanks a lot." I closed the notebook.

"Okay. That's probably enough for today. Should we meet next Sunday?"

"Sure. I want to know all about Chicago."

It was weirdest feeling to know that Gramps had done all kinds of things long before I was born and he had known all kinds of people I would never meet. He had people inside him like Giovanni who were always there even though Gramps only knew him for a couple of months. I guess it was lucky for us that Gramps met him. Otherwise, he would have been so homesick that maybe he would have gone right back to Italy. Then, he wouldn't have met my grandmother, my mom and Aunt Florence wouldn't be here, and neither would I.

Chapter Seven

Aunt Florence's Hook Shot

After Gramps and I finished our interview, I didn't quite know what to do since it was too early in the day for homework. I went out into the kitchen to see what my mom was up to. She was rolling out the dough for the greatest rolls in the world; crescent rolls.

"I'll help, Mom," I said.

"Okay." She finished rolling out a circle and then cut it into wedges.

I rolled the wedges from the wide end to the skinny part. I put each one on a tray.

"How was your interview?"

"Good. Gramps told me about saying goodbye to his mom."

"I haven't heard that story in years. When I was little he would talk about going to Italy."

"Gramps said he never saw his parents again."

"He didn't. By the time the Depression and World War Two were over both Grandpa and Grandma

Rossini were dead. Gramps went to see Aunt Sofia after the War." My mom had a second circle of dough ready. She cut the wedges and motioned to me.

I nodded. I was almost done with the first circle. "Did Aunt Sofia ever come here?"

"Once."

"What was that for?"

My mom handed me another tray since mine was full. She covered the rolls with a cloth. They had to rise again. "She came to see all of us."

"I know she's alive because she still writes to Gramps."

"Yes, she's alive. Her four children and seven grandchildren live in Italy."

"Do you think we could go over there to visit them?"

"Maybe someday."

When my mom said, "maybe someday" that really meant the conversation was over. The more I thought about it, the more I wanted to go to Italy. How could I get Gramps to go to Italy to see his sister?

When Aunt Florence got home she went downstairs to change her uniform and put her hat away. That was the routine every day she worked. I thought I heard her say hi to me before she went downstairs but I didn't say hi back because I wasn't really sure if that's what I heard.

Aunt Florence came upstairs and hung around in the kitchen with my mom. I could hear them talking as they filled the dishes with steaming mashed potatoes, gravy, and corn. My dad brought the rump roast over to his place and set it to the left of his plate. Once, when I was seven, I asked what part of the cow the rump was and everybody started laughing. When my dad finally told me that it was the rear end of the cow, I couldn't believe it.

"You mean their butt?" I asked. Thankfully, I didn't have any rump roast melting in my mouth when I asked or I would have spit it onto my plate. I decided right then and there that rump roast was not for me. I put aside my plate with the two slices of rump and didn't eat any more that night. Three weeks later we had a rump roast again and after my initial resistance, my nose sniffed the air, my mouth watered, and I decided it wouldn't hurt anything if I had one slice. One thing led to another, and pretty soon, I was eating like this rear end was what I'd been waiting for my whole life.

Well, that was five years ago and although I've

had to wrestle with myself more than once I have to admit that there aren't too many things that taste better than a cow's butt.

"Colette, get the rolls from your mother," my dad said.

"I'll take the rolls," I said. My mom handed me a basket with a linen napkin folded across the top.

I walked into the dining room with the basket. Gramps always sat across from me at the table and since he was already sitting in his spot, I walked over to him and opened the linen napkin so he could take a roll. He took one, grabbed the plate with the butter stick on it, sliced a generous chunk of butter off with his butter knife, and proceeded to butter his roll while putting his finger up to his lips and saying, "Shh."

"Yep, it's our little secret." I put the basket by my mom's place and went back out in the kitchen.

"Get the milk and water, would you, Colette?" my mom asked. She walked into the dining room carrying the mashed potatoes. Aunt Florence was in hot pursuit with the gravy and corn.

I poured milk for four of us and water for Gramps. We sat down and waited for Gramps to say the blessing. He liked to add to the usual "Bless Us Oh Lord," a bowed head "Thank you for my family." Then we all said, "Amen," blessed ourselves, and my dad said, "Let's eat."

Soon my plate filled up with cow's rump, mashed potatoes and gravy, corn, and a crescent roll. I loved Sunday dinner. We used our good dishes and silverware on Sundays along with linen napkins. It had an extra bonus too. I didn't have to wash the dishes because my mom was afraid I'd break one of them. She asked every Sunday if I minded if she and Aunt Florence did the dishes and I didn't argue, believe me.

"Colette, I can come to your game," Aunt Florence said. "I changed with another supervisor so I don't have to work that evening."

"That's great," I said. "I look forward to seeing you there." The words had just somersaulted out of my mouth and I couldn't explain it but I felt really happy. "What was your specialty shot?"

"I used to shoot a mean hook shot."

"More than once your hook shot won the game, Florence," Gramps said. He buttered a roll and winked at me.

"Maybe you could show me your moves, Aunt Florence," I said.

"Oh, I'm out of practice after so many years."

"Some things you never forget. Pass the rolls, please."

Aunt Florence plucked a roll out of the basket and

sailed it across the table with her right arm arced. I caught it in the air.

"Aunt Florence, that is a mean hook shot."

She actually giggled and I can say for a fact that in all my eleven and a half years in Red Wing, Minnesota I had never heard my aunt laugh out loud. Her laugh was kind of contagious since it sounded so high-pitched and almost musical. I couldn't help laughing and neither could Mom, Dad, and Gramps. We sat longer than usual that night at the table. As a rule I liked to be the first to excuse myself but with everybody talking and laughing I just didn't get around to it. Gramps was the first to leave since his TV shows were on Sunday nights.

My mom and Aunt Florence got busy doing the dishes while my dad cleared the table and put things away. Gramps "retired" to the living room and turned on the TV, settled into his chair, and waited. He loved to watch *The Lawrence Welk Show* on Saturday evenings but Sunday was his favorite for TV. He watched *Walt Disney* followed by *The Ed Sullivan Show* followed by the *Glen Campbell Good-time Hour.*

Sunday nights the whole family watched Ed, as I called him. After all, the Beatles had been on his show so how could I ever even think about missing it.

Tonight, for some reason, I didn't feel like watching *Walt Disney* with Gramps so I found myself meandering out to the kitchen even though it was my day of rest from the dishes.

"What are you guys doing now?"

"We're just finishing the pans. Want to help?" Aunt Florence asked.

I started rubbing the inside of the pan dry and then the outside. I kept thinking about how that crescent roll just flew across the table to me. I was going to ask about basketball when these words came out of my mouth, "Aunt Florence, do you like nursing?"

"I love nursing."

"Why do you love it?"

"Well, because I feel I'm helping people who are sometimes in the scariest, most vulnerable times in their lives. It makes me feel good."

"Did you always know you would love nursing?"

"No, I don't think I did."

"Did you know you wanted to be a nurse when you were my age?"

"No."

"What made you decide to be a nurse?"

Aunt Florence stepped over by the window and looked out. She started to say something and then stopped but her mouth was still slightly open. I couldn't take my eyes off my aunt.

"Florence, are you going to watch Ed Sullivan?" my mom asked. She hung up her apron in the pantry on the special hook for aprons.

"Yes, but first I'm going to answer Colette's question." I could barely hear her voice as she began speaking. "At a time when I was so frightened I didn't know what to do, a nurse showed me compassion. She held me as I cried and made me feel that she cared about me. I've never forgotten her."

I'm hardly the kind of person who's ever lost for words but this time I was. Since both Aunt Florence's and my mom's eyes were kind of wet like a drizzly summer rain, I simply didn't know what to say. So for once in my eleven and a half years of life, I kept my mouth shut. I stood there thinking I should say something to this revelation but then I was afraid that the drizzle would become a deluge and pretty soon I would be overcome by the moment and start crying about who knows what. No, it would be too weird of a Sunday to have Aunt Florence laughing so contagiously that everyone joined in, then have her admit she was frightened so badly that she wept, then actually see tears in her eyes, then have me crying with her. I just would not do it. I did the next best thing. I hugged her. It seemed like a perfectly natural thing to do.

Well, my mom hugged both of us and I felt as if I would suffocate so I was glad when through the group hug I heard the saving voice of my dad telling us *The Ed Sullivan Show* had started.

Chapter Eight

Mrs. Bosworth

The next day I leapt out of bed when the alarm went off. I couldn't wait to talk to Sally about the strange happenings of the night before. She was always at school early so I would probably find her on the playground.

"Bye, Mom," I yelled upstairs. "I'm going."

I walked so fast that I was almost running. As I rounded the corner, I saw Sally standing with two other girls. I didn't want to be rude and yell for just Sally like the other two girls didn't even count because I hated it when girls did that. Anyway, I couldn't very well whisk Sally away from the other two so I just kind of eased my way into the circle, saying hi to everyone and don't let me interrupt you. Everyone said hi.

Sally said, "Colette, I don't believe it, you're here before the bell rings."

"I just may do this every morning," I said. "Especially since it looks like you're having such pleasant conversation."

They all agreed the conversation was pleasant enough. After ten minutes of making fun of Mr. Mooney, the principal, and talking about the unfair expectations of our teachers, we moved on to who we thought the cutest boy in our class was. Just when we decided to vote since we had differences of opinion, the bell rang, and we all lined up to go into the school.

As we walked in, I said to Sally, "I have to talk to you."

"Okay. How about lunch?"

"Agreed."

We each went our separate ways to our classrooms. It was hard to pay attention during history because I kept thinking of how shocked Sally was going to be about Aunt Florence's laughing, crying, and hugging. I thought I heard someone say "Miss McGiver" but it sounded far away like it was a dream. Then I saw the sturdy shoes of Mrs. Bosworth standing next to my desk. She had her arms crossed and her light blue eyes were flashing. One thing that really made her mad was kids not listening to her.

"Miss McGiver, can you tell us what we were just discussing in class?"

"Um. We were discussing the difference between Athens and Sparta," I answered quickly.

After my answer Mrs. Bosworth's eyes actually

narrowed into a pair of slits. Her lips disappeared until all I could see was skinny eyes, a nose, and a chin. I knew all the kids were watching me but I didn't dare look around. My eyes were locked with my teacher's tight face.

"We finished history a half hour ago, Miss McGiver. Can you put your history book away and take out your math book?"

"Sure." I threw my history book in my desk and grabbed my math book in almost one motion.

"That's good of you."

The room was as still as the air before a bad summer storm so I started wondering if the class was going to hear about how learning was a privilege or that Mrs. Bosworth didn't care to waste her time on people who didn't want to learn. Waste of anything was sinful, she would say, but especially our God-given, not earned mind you, minds were a terrible thing to waste. I usually enjoyed listening to Mrs. Bosworth's lectures because they were directed at screwy boys who never did their homework. I really did like learning about, for instance, the differences between Athens and Sparta in ancient Greece and I dearly loved math so this was the first time Mrs. Bosworth had planted her sturdy shoes next to my desk.

"Do you think you can join us now?"

"Yes, I think so." I couldn't believe I was getting off without a lecture.

"Okay, then, let's look at the problem on the board. Who wants to finish it?"

Half the room's hands shot up in the air like they came right out of a cannon. We had learned after Mrs. Bosworth zeroed in on a specific kid, the best thing the other kids in the class could do was show her we were paying attention. Of course, the kid who she had yelled at always shot their hand in the air but she never called on them so I waved my hand in the air fully expecting someone else to be called on.

"Colette, go ahead."

I jumped out of my chair and walked up to the board. She couldn't have been too mad if she was back to my first name that quickly. We were working on our skills in addition, subtraction, multiplication, and long division. I added the column of about ten numbers, no problem, and went back to my seat. One of the other kids was soon up there doing another of the problems.

We still had reading to do before lunch. When the bell went off, we put away our books and papers, and waited to be dismissed.

"Remember, class, all of you come back to school tonight with your parents. I'll remind you again before you go home."

She really had a one-track mind sometimes. How could we possibly forget such a momentous occasion?

Okay, class, you're dismissed." I lined up by the door when Mrs. Bosworth stopped me. "Colette, wait a minute, will you?"

"Sure." I knew Sally would save a spot for me in the lunchroom but I wanted to have time to tell her the latest family news.

"Are you feeling okay?"

"I feel fine." I had never heard Mrs. Bosworth ask a kid how they were feeling. She assumed we were feeling fine and if we weren't it was our problem, not hers. She did not believe in mollycoddling students since she said we got enough of that at home and that was not her job. She took her job very seriously.

"You seem preoccupied, like something is bothering you."

"No, I'm okay. Just a little tired, that's all."

"I hope you would come to me if you needed to talk."

"I would, Mrs. Bosworth." I didn't want to hurt her feelings since she took her job so seriously and all, but she was the last person I would ever talk to. For one thing, she would probably tell my mom right away when the reason I had talked to her was because I didn't want my mom to know. Otherwise, I would have talked to my mom about it already and had no need to talk to Mrs. Bosworth. I suppose there were some desperate kids who just had to talk to someone and they didn't have a Sally in their life so there they were revealing their innermost thoughts and fears to their teacher. I decided right then and there that I would never just assume someone was trying to get in good with the teacher when the kid stayed after school because maybe they had no one else they could talk to.

"Okay, then, you can go."

"Thank you." I left the room. Maybe it really was true what the kids were saying about the birth of Mrs. Bosworth's grandson around Christmas; it had softened her up.

Sally had a place waiting for me at the lunch table. "Okay. Give. What d'you want to tell me?"

I started telling Sally about the emotional evening with Aunt Florence and she didn't interrupt me once. She just nodded her head and said, "Mm hmm" and "Interesting" over and over. I told her about Aunt Florence and my mom both starting to cry. I ended the story with the fact that Mom, Aunt Florence, and I had a group hug.

Sally laughed and said, "Good. Now you finally know what it's like to be in my family."

I said, "You poor little thing."

"Do you think this frightening time for your aunt has anything to do with Daniel?"

"That's what I wondered too." After I went upstairs the night before, all of a sudden I thought about Daniel. I was putting on my pajamas when Daniel came into my mind and there he stayed. I figured that whatever Aunt Florence was so misty-eyed about had something to do with Daniel.

"Finish your lunch so we can go outside," Sally said. "Hurry up."

I hurried as fast as I could and we went outside. The playground was asphalt so there really wasn't much to do. The younger girls played jump rope and a game with a ball called four square but the older girls usually just walked around talking.

"Don't look now at who's coming over," Sally said.

I looked up in time to see the Bloomer waving wildly just like I did when I tried every which way to get her to notice me down by the basket. She came running over. "Are you ready for the big game?" She clapped her hands.

"I guess."

"I'll pass to you, okay?"

"That would be great." I might as well be ready just in case.

"Are you going to practice after school?"

"Of course. I wouldn't miss practice."

"I'll see ya there then," Patty Bloomer said. She began walking back to her group of eighth grade girls. I watched her go for a minute and then turned back to Sally. I opened my mouth to say something about the Bloomer and her idea of accuracy in her passing game when I heard my name loud and clear. The Bloomer was waving madly again. "Colette, I want to tell you something."

"Okay, shoot."

"Try to get yourself open by the basket more often, would you? I can't pass if you're not open." Patty Bloomer turned away, this time for good, and strode purposefully towards the eighth graders.

The bell rang. Everyone lined up.

"Don't forget, tonight's the night," I said. "The big event."

"I haven't forgotten," Sally said.

"Save me a seat. I think we should go through this together."

"Agreed."

By the time I got home from practice at 5:30 pm, ate dinner, and did my homework, it was time to go back to school for the "big event."

Sally was already there so she patted the seat next to

her. I quickly sat down and my mom sat next to me. All the girls in our grade were there and the two sixth grade teachers since they were both woman. Mr. Mooney was in charge of the movie for the boys and dads.

"I'm so glad that you're all here tonight," Mrs. Bosworth said. She was standing on the stage next to a large portable white screen.

"I'm not," I whispered to Sally.

"We've been showing this film for many years but this is the first year we've shown it to the sixth grade class. We hope it's a good experience for all of you. We think it's an important step to come to school with your mothers, watch this film, and then go home and ask questions if you need to. So, why don't we get started?" Mrs. Bosworth nodded to the person standing by the projector. She walked to the side of the stage and turned off the lights.

The screen lit up with the words, "Becoming a Woman." The narrator began talking about growing up and how our bodies were going to change. And that was completely normal. Even our skin changed, the narrator said. It became oily.

I couldn't believe my eyes but there was a pimple on the screen and that pimple was getting bigger and bigger. It became what can only be described as a giant pimple – it literally filled the screen.

"O my gawd," Sally said. "It's huge!" She giggled and poked me.

Mrs. Reynolds gave Sally a look that could kill. "Do we have to separate the two of you?" she asked.

I covered my mouth and looked straight ahead. I couldn't look at Sally. It took every ounce of my strength to keep from laughing.

The narrator talked on and on about our bodies growing and changing. The screen showed hair growing on some girl's arm, then in her armpits, and then down there. Yuck! I was done. I decided right then and there that I really didn't care what happened to my body or anyone else's. I couldn't watch it anymore. I chose a corner of the screen that was plain white and had nothing growing on it and I stared. I started humming.

"Colette, you're humming *Battle Hymn of the Republic*," Sally said. "Stop it or I'm going to wet my pants."

"Sorry." I didn't even know I was humming much less why I was humming that. But I didn't dare take my eyes off the corner of the screen. Thankfully, the film was only fifteen minutes long and I was able to think about my interview with Gramps and the big game coming up.

The lights were turned back on and there was Mrs. Bosworth smiling and trying to look very sincere. "Girls, do you have any questions?" Mrs. Bosworth asked.

I was elated no one raised their hands.

"Okay, then, you are dismissed."

Sally and I stood outside, saying nothing. Sally finally broke the silence. "We'll have to discuss all of this tomorrow."

"Agreed."

"Why were you humming *The Battle Hymn of the Republic?* I wanted to get up and march." Sally started marching.

She really was such a riot. "I don't know why I was humming that. It just came out. I'm so glad we sat together, Sal, or I wouldn't have made it through."

"Me either."

"I thought the whole film was very interesting," my mom said. "Didn't you?"

"It was interesting all right," I said. "Quite the experience. Please promise me you'll never bring it up again."

My mom and I walked home. I took a bath, washed my hair, and put on my pajamas. I towel-dried my hair and thought about what I should do next. Rolling up my thick, unruly hair in brush rollers with the picks holding each roller tight to the scalp was out of the question because I couldn't sleep a wink all night. It had to be a dire emergency for me to wear rollers to bed. I brushed my hair about 50 times and hoped it wouldn't be sticking out all over in the morning. Maybe I would have to wear a bun like Aunt Florence after all.

I thought about how I could find out who the mysterious Daniel was. Maybe Aunt Florence's boyfriend really was named Daniel and he dumped her and broke her heart until a wonderful nurse hugged her while she cried.

It could have happened that way I suppose, but as I said before, my mom said the boyfriend's name wasn't Daniel and why was Aunt Florence with a nurse anyway? It just didn't make any sense. Where would she have seen a nurse? In a Dr.'s office? Or a hospital? Was she sick years ago?

Anyway, I knew she didn't have any disease now. She never called in sick for work because she never was sick. Colds or flu germs did not find Aunt Florence, or maybe they did and she just repelled them immediately in her business-like way. And then they found their way to the rest of us, and we coughed, sneezed, and blew our noses until Aunt Florence made comments like, "I suppose we're going to need more tissues. It looks like we're out. Tsk, tsk."

I decided to just go to bed since there wasn't anything else to do so I yelled downstairs to my mom that I was going to sleep. I turned off the light. I thought for a while about what the big game would be like and whether I would play and whether we would win.

I closed my eyes to picture myself shooting the winning hook shot and must have fallen asleep because the next thing I knew the sun had risen, the birds were chirping, and my alarm pierced my eardrums with its insistent chiming.

Chapter Nine

Grandma Rose

The week flew by as Gramps always said. I practiced basketball after school until dinner every night. The practices were more intense since the big game was almost here. We had scrimmage games where we played each other. Coach Brennan really got into it. He blew his whistle, yelled out plays, and ran up and down the court.

I liked it because I wasn't always playing with the Bloomer. I got to play with the eighth grade starters. Klein was another forward and she could really pass the ball. It was wonderful to wait by the basket and have the pass actually come right to me. Schmit was one of our best guards and she liked to block my shots. She sure didn't let you get an easy lay-up. You had to work for it against her. I especially liked playing with Doyle since she was the best player on the team. She could dribble, she could pass, she could shoot, and she could rebound. Plus, she was our jump ball person. Sometimes, I just watched in awe.

After dinner every night, I worked on my story about Gramps. I had gone to the library and found a book about Ellis Island. There was a picture of a man having his eyelids pulled down just like Gramps had described. I imagined Gramps in the big noisy room filled with people. It amazed me that he had been there.

Sunday came and we did our usual going to church and then eating at the diner. Gramps and I had our date set for one o'clock in the sunroom just like the week before. I had my notebook ready with questions about Chicago, my Grandma Rose, and then how he got to Red Wing, Minnesota.

Gramps waited for me in the sunroom. I walked in and sat in the loveseat. "Here we are again, Gramps."

"Here we are again."

I opened my notebook. "I think we left off at you going to Chicago."

"Yes. I left New York and took the train to Chicago. Cousin Beto was happy to see me. He told me to learn English and get my high school diploma. He signed me up for English lessons right away. He said otherwise I could be taken advantage of. The day I got my high school diploma was wonderful."

"Did you work too?"

"I did day work. I would take jobs for the day; anything they had available. A lot of the jobs were laying railroad tracks in the city. There were over 2000 miles of track so I got to know parts of Chicago very well."

"How long did you live with Cousin Beto?"

"For a year. Then I rented a room from a woman named Angella. I lived with her until Rose and I were married."

"How did you meet Grandma Rose?"

"On Saturdays I delivered prescriptions for Mr. Rheinberger who owned a pharmacy. One day, I couldn't find the street I was looking for and I asked a lovely young woman for directions."

"That must have been my grandma."

"It was. I can still see every movement of her face and hands. She had the most beautiful slate blue eyes I had ever seen. For me, it was truly love at first sight." Gramps smiled. "I walked by her house every couple of days trying to see her again. Finally, a month later, I saw her again. She introduced herself as Rosemary O'Keefe and said I could call on her on Sundays."

"Is that what you did?"

"Yes. I spent most of my Sunday afternoons with Rose and her family."

"For how long?"

"For two years. They called it courting in those days."

"Did her family like you?"

"Her mother, Marie, liked me. Sean and Liam, her two brothers, didn't pay much attention. Rose's father, Paddy, wasn't too sure of me. I had to win him over. When he realized that I would never do anything to hurt his daughter, we became great friends. I can still picture him sitting in front of the radio. He listened to all the mystery shows. There was one called *The Shadow* but his favorite was *Sherlock Holmes*. Everyone had to be quiet so Paddy could hear all the sound effects."

"He sounds fun."

"He was fun. He said at least I went to Mass every Sunday even if I wasn't Irish."

"You still do, Gramps."

"Mass has always been important to me. Paddy liked that. And he liked the fact that I became an American citizen. I asked Paddy for Rose's hand before I asked her to marry me. On November 3, 1928 Rose and I were married. It was the most wonderful day of my life."

"Where did you live?"

"With Paddy and Marie. I still had a year of pharmacy school left and Rose had to quit her job as a secretary after we got married. That's the way things were in those days. Married woman couldn't work. So Rose helped her mother at home and thought of ways she could make a little money. It was hard for her."

"Did you keep delivering prescriptions?"

"On Saturdays. Mr. Rheinberger had encouraged me to go to pharmacy school. He told me that someday we could be partners if I became a pharmacist. I planned on working for him until I could buy into the business. When the stock market crashed in 1929, we didn't realize what it meant for a long time."

"Did you lose your job?"

"Not right away. But people couldn't pay for their prescriptions so they either didn't get the medicine they needed or Mr. Rheinberger told them to pay when they got the money. He had a stack of IOU's in the back of the pharmacy.

"Mr. Rheinberger taught me how to make leather mittens for the cold like he had when he was growing up in Germany. After we had ten pairs made, I would go out in the streets and sell them for a dime apiece. We split the money so we each got a nickel. In July, 1930, Mr. Rheinberger told me he was going to close up completely. He said he didn't want to owe any more money."

"What'd you do then?"

"I had been looking for any day work I could find

but so were hundreds of other men. Mr. Rheinberger told me about a pharmacy with a soda fountain for sale in a place called Red Wing, Minnesota. He said I could probably get it really cheap with the state of the economy."

"So that's how you ended up in Red Wing."

"Yes."

"Did Grandma Rose want to move?"

"She was sad. Paddy suggested that Rose and I take the Great Northern train to Red Wing to look at the business and the town. Rose was expecting your mother at the time. We knew if we didn't travel right then she wouldn't be able to for months. Rose was quiet on the train but once we got to Minnesota, she loved it. She had all kinds of plans. She liked the town and we both thought it would be a good place to raise a family."

"Were you glad to leave Chicago?"

"I didn't like leaving certain people but I had never planned on living in a big city. I lived there because that's where the jobs were. Rose's parents, Paddy and Marie, said they would help us buy the store. We waited until after your mother was born. She arrived on December 28, 1930. I left for Red Wing in January, 1931. Rose and Paddy came a month later."

"I bet you were happy to see them, Gramps."

"I was so happy. I promised Rose I would make it work for us. She corrected me and said that the two of us would make it work. So it became a great partnership."

"Did she help at the store?"

"She jumped right in. She did the bookkeeping and loved working in the soda fountain. But it was the Depression and I found myself in the same situation Mr. Rheinberger had been in. Not enough money to pay the bills. Rose had the idea of giving free Cokes or phosphates to people while they waited for their prescriptions. It saved us running to people's houses and while they waited, sometimes they bought ice cream or something else. I always said Rose made the business grow."

"How smart."

"She was very smart. It was simple idea but it made a huge difference."

I had closed my notebook halfway through our conversation just like the week before. I liked watching Gramps face when he talked about people in his past. His whole face got kind of soft looking when he talked about Grandma Rose. He must have really loved her a lot.

"I think I have all I need for my paper, Gramps. But that doesn't mean we can't talk like this again."

"Sure, anytime."

"I wish I would have known Grandma Rose."

"She would have loved you as much as I do, Bella. Come here and give me a kiss."

I snorted like I always did when he called me that.

Gramps laughed. "You're funny. I'll see you at dinner."

What was amazing to me was that people really do live on through other people. Even though Giovanni had died almost 50 years ago, he still had a place in Gramp's heart. I wondered if 50 years from now I'd be telling my grandkids about the Bloomer and Sally. And maybe they'd be telling their grandkids about me. One thing was certain though; Gramps would always be with me.

Chapter Ten

The Hospital

Monday, after practice, Coach Brennan gave us a pep talk about how proud he was of all of us. He said to just get out there at the championship game and play like we had all season. If we lost there was nothing to be ashamed of because that was the game; someone had to win and someone had to lose. He said he had enjoyed coaching us all year and he was going to miss us because we were the greatest bunch of girls he had ever coached. His eyes filled with tears. Then Coach Brennan cleared his throat and thankfully, his eyes went back to normal. He dismissed us early and told us to have a good dinner, get a good night's sleep, and he would see us tomorrow at 6:00 pm.

I grabbed my book bag and left the gym. To my surprise my mom pulled up in the car. She honked and motioned for me to get in. My mom didn't believe in honking at people when she picked them up so I tried to swallow but I couldn't; my mouth was too dry.

"Get in, Colette. Gramps had a stroke."

I threw my book bag into the back seat. My heart pounded and it hurt to breathe. All I could think of was that Gramps was going to die and I would never see him again. I couldn't stand the thought. I squeaked out, "Is he alive?"

"Yes, he's alive. He's in the hospital and they're running tests right now. Florence and your dad are with him."

"What happened?"

"I came home from school and Gramps was lying on the living room floor. I ran over and saw he was breathing but he didn't open his eyes when I yelled, 'Dad.' So I called the ambulance and then I called your father."

I pictured poor Gramps lying on the floor all by himself, maybe for a long, long time, and none of us even knowing he was there. I wiped my eyes because I didn't want my tears to escape and start streaming down my cheeks.

"And then I didn't know what to do. If I should call Florence at work or call at school and have someone go get you or if I should sit on the floor next to Gramps. I decided I'd sit and hold his hand. I sat on the floor and held his hand until the ambulance came."

"That's what I would have done too, Mom."

"Now you realize Gramps is going to look different than he did this morning."

"How?"

"The left side of his face droops and his left arm and leg are limp."

We walked into the hospital and stopped at the information desk.

"Excuse me, can you tell me where Mr. Rossini is?" my mom asked.

"Let's see, Mr. Rossini. He's still in the Emergency Room. There's a waiting room down there," the woman said. She looked up from under her very red, large, ratted hair. None of her hairs moved even a fraction of an inch when she moved her head. I wondered how she could sleep on it. Did she just put more hairspray on when she got up in the morning? "You can take that hallway and just follow the signs," the woman said as she pointed to the hallway on the left. Her red lips kind of grimaced and revealed some very large teeth.

As my mom and I walked towards the hallway to the left, I glanced back at the information lady. The phone rang and she picked it up efficiently, looking just the right amount of serious. She answered the person's question and then hung up. She put two of her fingers in her mouth for a second, licked them and smoothed down a couple of hairs she thought were out of place. She reached under the information desk, pulled out her purse, and took out some red lipstick and a small mirror. She put more lipstick on, pursed her lips together, took out a tissue, and puckered her lips together into the tissue. Her lips didn't seem any redder after the new lipstick but I didn't think any lips could get redder than the information lady's. She looked over at my staring eyes and winked. If it hadn't been for Gramps being down in the emergency room, I would have laughed.

We found Aunt Florence and my dad down in the Emergency Room. Gramps hadn't opened his eyes yet but Aunt Florence said that wasn't unusual with a stroke. He also had had something called an EEG. That was short for a really long, hard to pronounce word. The word just rolled off Aunt Florence's tongue. No problem.

Mom, Dad, and Aunt Florence talked about my Grandma Rose and how hard it was on Gramps when she was sick. She had had a stroke but also had a lot of problems with her heart. I lost interest after a while since all of this happened before I was born. While they talked I said a little prayer, which I didn't do often, and asked God not to take our Gramps away from us.

One of the nurses came out to talk to us. She knew Aunt Florence since this was where Aunt Florence worked. "We're going to move your father to the ICU now," she said. "His blood pressure has stabilized and his other vitals are fine. He's still not responding but you know that can change quickly."

"Are they going to do more tests?" my mom asked.

"Not right now. I think the plan is to get him to ICU, put him on a monitor, and watch him carefully. The doctor will come out to talk to you before he leaves," the nurse said. She turned back and said, "Sorry about this, Florence."

The doctor came out and told us pretty much the same information the nurse had. He added that it was hard to tell how extensive the stroke was and it became a wait and see approach. I guess everyone was supposed to watch Gramps for any kind of response. He said something about some kind of medicine to keep the blood from clotting and another to keep the blood pressure down. Aunt Florence nodded. How can you live in the same house with someone and not even know that they knew all about basketball and special kinds of medications to prevent blood from clotting and others that kept the blood pressure down?

The nurse said, "ICU is ready for Mr. Rossini."

When I saw Gramps being wheeled out, I felt like

crying. I swallowed hard and blinked my eyes a couple of times. Gramps had tubes running from two places in his good right arm to dripping glass bottles hanging on poles. A person was pushing a big green tank with a bottle attached to it. There was bubbling water in the bottle and a tube connected to it. Aunt Florence said it was oxygen and that Gramps needed it right now. The other end of the tube went into a mask that fit tightly over his nose and mouth. The oxygen hissed as the bed moved. Gramp's eyes were closed and I could tell when I looked closer that the left side of his face kind of hung down a little. His skin looked whiter than it had ever been even in the longest winter.

Anyway, I didn't know where to touch him since he had the bad side now and the other side was filled with tubes so I just walked next to him. A machine beeped out the rhythm of his heart and made this up and down line on a long skinny piece of paper. One end of a lot of wires connected to the machine and the other end was under Gramp's hospital gown. The paper just kept printing and printing. I found myself watching the paper and being happy that his heart was beating away.

Gramps was upstairs in the ICU or Intensive Care Unit in no time, and boy, were the nurses up there busy. We stayed outside the room while they got Gramps in his bed and hooked him up to their own beeping heart machine and oxygen tank. All I could see was two pairs of sturdy white nurse's shoes moving under the curtain. As the curtain slid aside with authority, there was Gramps looking small and white in his hospital bed.

"Hi, Florence," the nurse said. Then she turned to the rest of us. "My name is Maggie and I'm Mr. Rossini's nurse. Are you all family?"

"Yes," my mom said.

"You can all go in for five minutes. I'm going to check the orders and I'll be around if you have any questions. Okay?"

"Is he going to be all right?" I asked.

"He's stable right now and we're watching him carefully," Maggie said.

I had been thinking about this since my mom picked me up so I had to ask. "How can a person like Gramps be so healthy and then all of a sudden he can't walk, talk, or even move?"

"It's always a shock how quickly things can happen," Maggie said. "Hang in there." She squeezed my arm.

We walked over to Gramp's bed. My legs felt kind of heavy and, as funny as it sounds, so did my heart. I could feel it like a large presence in my chest. My mom rubbed Gramp's good arm and said, "Dad, we're all here." She stopped and I looked up and saw her wipe under her eyes. My dad put his arm around her and then he put his other arm around me.

"You can talk to Gramps if you want to," my dad said. "They told us they don't know what a person understands when they're in a coma."

I really didn't know what to say. It wasn't like usual when I said something and Gramps patted my arm or laughed or his eyes twinkled. I swallowed even though I didn't have any saliva in my mouth. "Gramps, it's Colette," I said. The words sounded strange since there was no response from Gramps. I wished I had the perfect words to make him open his eyes.

Aunt Florence had stayed back to talk with Maggie, nurse to nurse. She came into the room now and stood with the rest of us. I liked her being with us since she was in her nurse uniform and she seemed to know all about everything they would do for Gramps.

"Anything new?" my mom asked.

"Nothing new. We just have to wait and see," Aunt Florence said.

Nurse Maggie came into the room, looked at the monitors, and then looked at Gramps. "Why don't you go all to the cafeteria and get something to eat? We'll be in here for awhile."

We trudged down to the cafeteria and looked at

the choices of food. I usually was so hungry after basketball practice that I even had second helpings but for some reason, even though it was 7:30 pm, I didn't feel hungry. My dad bought a huge hamburger for the two of us with a big plate of french fries. Mom and Aunt Florence just had a cup of coffee each.

"One of us should stay tonight," Aunt Florence said. She sat down at the table and put both her hands around the coffee cup.

"I'll stay," my mom said.

"I think I should tonight, Gemma. I'm not working tomorrow." Aunt Florence took a sip of steaming coffee, then set her cup back on the table with her two hands around it.

"Maybe that would be better. We'll take turns."

"You can stay tomorrow night."

"I'll take my turn too," my dad said.

"Thank you, John," Aunt Florence said. "But you have to work during the day. Our jobs are more flexible."

"I don't work Sundays so I'll plan on staying Saturday night."

"Thank you," my mom said. My parents looked at each other for what seemed to be a long time and there was something passing between them. They drew strength from each other, my mom had told me recently. It seemed like my dad was just giving my mom all the strength he had.

"What's family for? We'll get through this." My dad patted my mom's arm again like he'd been doing and then he looked at me. "You better eat, Colette, or you won't be able to shoot a basket tomorrow."

"Much less a hook shot," Aunt Florence said. "Too bad I don't have a crescent roll with me or we could practice." She arced her right arm around and everybody laughed. It wasn't the fun laughing like we had done at the dinner table the week before but I could feel my heart lightening a little bit.

"Maybe I *will* have some of the hamburger, Dad."

"That's my girl," my dad said. "I knew I'd have trouble finishing this giant burger myself. Anybody else want some?"

Aunt Florence and my mom both shook their heads no.

I had forgotten all about my big game tomorrow. "Don't think you have to come to my game," I said. "I don't want Gramps waking up and there's nobody there to talk to."

"We'll work it out, Colette. No need for you to worry," my mom said.

"I could take my turn too," I said.

"I think you probably could but I know the hospital wouldn't let you. They're not supposed to even let anyone under twelve in the hospital rooms," Aunt Florence said.

"Did they let me because of you?"

"No, they didn't ask so I didn't say anything."

Here I had always thought Aunt Florence with her starched uniform and her perfectly placed nursing hat would follow the hospital rules no matter what. "That's what I do at school too. If they don't ask, it's their problem," I said.

"Exactly," Aunt Florence said as she gulped down the last of her coffee. "I'm going to go to the ICU for a minute and check if there's anything new. Then I'd better go home to change if I'm going to stay overnight."

"Should we come now too?" my mom asked.

"No need. Don't hurry. I'll wait up there until you come up." Aunt Florence pushed the chair out from the table, stood up, and slung her purse over her shoulder. She strode out of the cafeteria quickly, stopping for a minute to talk with another nurse.

"The other nurses seem to like Aunt Florence," I said. I dipped my french fry in the small pile of ketchup on my plate and then bit into it. It really tasted good.

"She's been here a long time," my mom said.

We talked a little bit about everything but what

was really on our minds. That was how bad Gramp's stroke really was, how long he was going to be in the hospital, if he was going to wake up, if he was going to be the same, and my question, when was he coming home?

Gramps looked exactly the same as he had when we left him except for one thing. He had another tube added to his arsenal of tubes. It went into his bladder and drained pee from the bladder into a bag on the side of the bed.

"At least Gramps doesn't have many more places they can put tubes," I said.

"Oh, you'd be surprised," Maggie, the nurse, said. "Wouldn't she, Florence?" She looked over at Aunt Florence and they both chuckled real softly. I decided right then and there that although my curiosity usually made me ask all kinds of questions, this time I simply was not that curious. I didn't want to know where the other places were that they could put tubes.

"Any more questions?" Aunt Florence said. She smiled at me and I remembered that she had thought I was old enough to stay overnight with Gramps even though I technically wasn't old enough to even be in the room.

"No more questions."

"I'm going to go home now. I'll be back in about

an hour. Colette, you can come with me if it's okay with your mom and dad."

"You don't have to stay. Go home and try to relax," my mom said.

"I guess I will." I felt so tired that all I wanted to do was lie on my bed, read a little while I listened to the Beatles, or maybe just go to sleep. Thankfully, I didn't have any homework to do. Mrs. Bosworth said since everyone planned on going to the big game she wouldn't give us homework for two nights.

Aunt Florence and I rode home and she asked me all kinds of questions about my basketball team and the Bloomer especially. The Bloomer was always a great conversation piece. I told her about the Bloomer telling me to get more open so she could pass to me. Aunt Florence laughed in her contagious way.

We pulled up in front of our dark house and I said, "Thanks for the ride."

"You're very welcome."

"Aunt Florence, Gramps is going to be okay, isn't he?

"I hope so, I really hope so."

Chapter Eleven

Knock 'em Dead

It was hard to sleep because I kept thinking about Gramps in his hospital bed. I wondered if he thought about anything while he was in the coma and then I wondered if he was going to come out of it. I couldn't stand the thought of this being Gramps forever.

Mainly I hoped he'd still have the same personality because my Gramps was just about perfect the way he was.

When my mom and dad came home, they both stood in my bedroom doorway since my light was off.

"I'm awake," I said.

"Can I turn on the light?" my mom asked. The light came on like a blazing sunrise. My mom sat on my bed and my dad stood next to her. "Are you okay?" she asked.

"I'm okay. How's Gramps?"

"No change."

"I don't have to go to my game tomorrow. I don't really want to anyway."

"You're going to your game and we'll be cheering for you just like Gramps would be if he could," my dad said.

"We'll just have to take it one day at a time," my mom said. "Try to sleep now. You have school tomorrow. I love you, Colette."

"I love you too, Mom."

The next morning I wanted to stay in bed but my dad wouldn't let me. My mom had left for the hospital before my dad woke me. Aunt Florence could come home to sleep after my mom relieved her in Gramp's room.

I thought I'd be running the last two blocks to school and then scrambling through the doorway as the bell was ringing. Not that I didn't have plenty of experience doing that in the past but I had gotten out the habit in the last week or so. Just as I was going out the door my dad asked me if I wanted a ride. He must have known that on this morning I didn't have the energy to run to school and arrive gasping for breath as the bell was ringing.

"I'm going to stop at the hospital and then go to work," my dad said. "You don't have practice after school, do you?"

"No."

"Okay. Someone will pick you up at school. What time do you have to be back?"

"I have to be at the gym at 6:00 pm."

"Someone will bring you back then."

We arrived at school just in the nick of time. Everyone had lined up by the doors waiting for the bell to ring. Sally waved to me and I ran over.

"Back to your old…"

I didn't wait for Sally to finish. "Gramps had a stroke yesterday."

"Oh, I'm sorry. Is he okay?"

"We don't know. He's not even opening his eyes."

The bell rang and we filed into the school. Sally and I parted ways with the promise of meeting at lunch.

Mrs. Bosworth told me she was sorry about my grandfather as soon as I walked into my homeroom.

I thanked Mrs. Bosworth and went to my desk. The morning passed quickly since I worked hard at paying attention. When I kept looking at the clock five minutes seemed like an hour so I even raised my hand a few times and pretended I was really into the subject. All I was really thinking about was whether Gramps had woken up. I kept hoping and hoping that he had.

I was first in line when the bell rang for lunch. Sally had a place for me at the lunch table right across from her. I told her all about Gramps with his oxygen mask, special drips, tubes going into his good arm, wires connected to his chest and the monitor, the tube draining his pee into a bag, and the worst of all; Gramps just lying there not talking or moving.

Sally listened but every so often made noises like, "ohh." She put her hand to her mouth a couple of times.

We went out to the playground and soon we were in the before school group of girls. We had discussed the movie "Becoming a Woman" for the whole previous week. The subject came up again. Everyone but me loved all the gross details. I told the group that there was a reason why I had looked at the corner of the screen during the whole movie. I didn't want any nasty pictures in my mind. Sally made me hum *Battle Hymn of the Republic* so we could all laugh. Sally marched. We finally decided that the giant pimple said it all so there wasn't much else to say.

We were still debating who the cutest boy in our grade was so the conversation became loud and lively within a few minutes. It wasn't that there were so many to choose from but they each had their good and bad points. After we were done with our sixth grade class we would decide who the cutest boy in the whole school was. At the rate we were going, we wouldn't even start debating that until September or October.

"See ya at the game," Sally said. She waved as we went to our separate classrooms. "The whole family's going."

My dad picked me up after school and we drove to the hospital. I learned there hadn't been much change in Gramps other than my mom thinking he tried to squeeze her hand when she talked to him. My mom would be sleeping there tonight and then we'd work out who would sleep there tomorrow night.

"You know all of us would be at the game if Gramps wasn't in the hospital," my dad said. We were stopped at the stoplight. His eyebrows were kind of pushed together.

"I know, Dad. It's okay, it really is." I didn't want him to think that I would be upset in any way if none of them came. After all, they hadn't missed a game all season. After I got home from each one of my games, Gramps, Dad, and I would go through a play-by-play rerun of the whole game. Each of us gave our own commentary on how this or that play could have been different, how often someone was open under the basket, how often someone took a bad shot, how to steal the ball from the other team, what my team did well, and, of course, what I did well. The commentary took well over an hour and it usually ended up with Gramps guffawing and slapping my back over some crazy play.

My dad parked the car in the parking lot across from the hospital and shut off the engine.

Gramps lay in the same bed in the ICU. My mom and Aunt Florence were talking seriously to each other.

"How's Gramps?" I asked. They both shook their heads. "How long does it usually take with a stroke for the person to open their eyes and talk?"

"Everyone is so different but, of course the sooner the person responds, the better," Aunt Florence said.

I learned that Gramp's stroke had been caused by his blood pressure getting too high. The high pressure caused one of the blood vessels in his brain to burst. They had done something called a spinal tap to see if there was bleeding in the brain. The doctor sticks a needle in your back and somehow he can tell what's going on in the brain. They also did another EEG to see if there was activity in the brain. Gramp's brain had activity. If there's no activity, that's really a bad sign.

Gramps had prided himself on never going to the doctor for anything. Aunt Florence was always after him to have a regular yearly checkup, to which he would reply, "Why? I'm fit as a fiddle." Another source of his pride was the fact that he took no medications. Gramps was not a bragging sort of person but he sure loved to brag about that. "I don't even take an aspirin," he would say. Aunt Florence tried to tell him that didn't mean he didn't need a yearly physical but he seemed to think that's exactly what taking no medications meant.

Anyway, Gramps always won the arguments since Aunt Florence would give up and say something like, "I can't make you go to the doctor." Gramps would heartily agree with her and thank her for seeing things his way. As it turns out if Gramps had gone to the doctor even once a year, they would have caught the high blood pressure, put him on medication, and maybe even prevented the stroke. The nurses said he had probably had high blood pressure for years.

I stared at Gramp's face as hard as I could while the rest of them talked. His right eyelid fluttered and opened a tiny bit. I grabbed my dad's arm and pointed to Gramp's eyes. My dad motioned to my mom and Aunt Florence. They stopped talking. "Hi, Gramps," I said as I squeezed his right hand. I felt a little movement of his fingers. But the best thing of all happened next because he opened his right eye all the way. The two of us locked our black, where-are-the-pupil eyes to each other.

"Dad, you had a stroke," Aunt Florence said. "You're in Intensive Care at the hospital."

Gramps didn't say anything; he just looked at all of us. Sometimes after a stroke the person couldn't talk, my dad told me. I hoped and hoped that Gramps would be able to talk.

My mom had gone to get the nurse and nurse Maggie came right in. "Mr. Rossini, blink if you hear me."

Gramps moved his eyelid a little.

"Okay, good, squeeze your granddaughter's hand."

Gramps squeezed a little harder this time. It was a definite squeeze.

"Ouch, Gramps," I said. "You'd beat me arm wrestling, that's for sure."

Because of his stroke, when Gramps tried to smile it was a little crooked. I moved out of the way so someone else could squeeze his hand. My dad was on the same side of the bed as me and he stepped right into the space I had moved out of. He put his hand over Gramp's hand and said, "We're here with you, Antonio."

The nurse asked Gramps a few other questions and his eyelid closed again. "He needs to sleep now," Nurse Maggie said.

We walked out of the room and stood there for a while, none of us knowing quite what to do. Finally my dad said that I better eat or I wouldn't be able to play basketball.

This time I ate the whole cheeseburger and french fries myself. My mom and Aunt Florence each had a sandwich with some soup. We sat with our spirits lifted because Gramps had opened his eyes, looked at us, and squeezed my hand.

Aunt Florence told us that Gramps wasn't out of the woods yet. A lot of things could happen including swelling in the brain or even another stroke. The nurses had already given him some blood from a total stranger who just donated it to be nice. They had to check all kinds of things in Gramp's blood including making sure the medications were the right amount. The more I thought about it, the more I wondered how anybody's body could keep track of all the things it had to do in a day, an hour, or a minute for that matter.

We went back upstairs to the ICU so I could say goodbye before the big game. After I got off the elevator, I automatically turned to the right without even giving it a thought and there was the ICU.

They had changed Gramps' position and had him sitting straighter in the bed. He looked more like himself that way even though his eyes were closed again. I wanted to tell him that even when I was at the game I'd be thinking about him but it was hard to talk to someone with their eyes closed so I didn't say anything. All of a sudden I felt this need to tell him all kinds of things like how much I liked going to Sunday breakfast with him even though we went to church first and how much I liked watching Ed with him on Sunday nights and how I could never ever remember him getting mad at me and how I loved hearing about Ellis Island and Grandma Rose and how I really did like being called Bella even though I turned up my nose at it. I stood there like I didn't have anything to say because what I wanted to say was so much that I didn't have the words for it.

"See ya tomorrow, Gramps. I'm going to my game now but I'll be thinking about you."

Gramps opened his good eye about halfway and then he tried to say something. I didn't need to ask him what he was saying. Before every basketball game he always said, "Knock 'em dead, Colette" as I was walking out the front door and I always turned around and said, "I won't be that hard on them."

"I won't be that hard on them," I said. "Don't worry. I'll remember every play so I can tell you all about it."

"Time to go," my dad said.

"Okay. Bye, Gramps." I kissed his bad cheek.

"Bye," Gramps said. It didn't quite sound like it used to, it was more like ba but I didn't care. Gramps understood what we said and tried to talk back.

Chapter Twelve

The Big Game

My dad dropped me off at the basketball court at 6:00 pm. I ran down to the locker room to change into my basketball uniform. We didn't have full uniforms like the boys did but I liked mine all the same. We had really cool shirts with our names on the back and a number. My number was twelve and although it wasn't my favorite number, it had begun to grow on me halfway through the season.

To finish my uniform, I wore a pair of cutoff jeans. They were my lucky shorts and I couldn't play basketball without them. Only once did I play a game without my cutoffs because they were in the wash. It was the worst game of my life and I couldn't even make a lay-up. The Bloomer had even passed me a couple of passes down by the basket that I caught and should have easily scored. Instead, my first shot went right over the hoop to the other side missing the basket completely. My second shot kind of hopped around the rim like it couldn't decide what to do. It fell to the floor, bounced over a guard on the other team, and then it landed squarely on the Bloomer's chest. She got so excited that she drove for the basket and made a nice little lay-up. Two points for the Bloomer and the team. Well, I tell you, I got so flustered that I didn't take another shot the rest of the game.

I said hi to the girls in the locker room and pulled my cutoffs out of the bag. They had been washed for a couple of weeks since the last game but I would have worn them dirty, believe me. I quickly changed into my number twelve basketball shirt and my lucky shorts.

"Isn't this exciting?" The Bloomer came running over. "I just can't believe it. The two years I'm on the team we go to the city championship. I must be the lucky star."

The Bloomer hugged me. "I just don't know what I'm going to do without you next year."

"I'll miss you too." I was surprised at the words that rolled out of my mouth but I never said anything like that unless I meant it so I guess I was going to miss the Bloomer after all.

I went upstairs, grabbed a basketball, and ran over to where members of the team were practicing.

The coach trotted over. "Okay, girls, line up for our practice. Everybody move into position."

We lined up in three lines so we could practice doing lay-ups from the right side, the left side, and down the middle. Then each of us had to shoot ten freethrows.

I finished my freethrows and ran to the sideline. Before I sat down, I looked up in the stands. There was my dad waving his hat like Gramps always did. Sitting next to him was Aunt Florence smiling like a Cheshire cat.

Sally and her family sat a couple of rows behind my dad and Aunt Florence, or at least Sally was sitting. Mr. and Mrs. Reynolds were nodding with grimaces on their faces to the people around them and it looked like they were saying, "Pardon me." They had thought ahead this time because Joe and Eric couldn't have been farther away from each other.

Coach Brennan told us to gather round. "All right, girls, this is it. We've been working for this all year. There are only two teams here tonight and you're one of them. I'm proud of each and every one of you. Now, go out there and give it your heart like you always do. Starters are Lynch, Schmit, and Henderson as guards and Doyle, Gustafson, and Klein as forwards. Okay, let's say a prayer."

We put our right hands in the middle and held on while we said the "Our Father." Then the coach said,

"Lord, thank you for bringing us to this point." The gong sounded.

The tallest girl on our team was Shannon Doyle so she was our jump ball person. She ran, clapping her hands, to the circle in the middle. The ref blew his whistle, then bent one knee while he catapulted the ball straight up in the air. Doyle jumped up and tipped the ball to one of our team.

I perched on the edge of my seat so I wouldn't miss a dribble. Our team passed a lot and kept moving until we got someone close to the basket. That some-one was Doyle. She was open right by the basket and she tipped in an easy one. Everybody breathed a sigh of relief because it meant the game was really under-way. The ball went to the other side and St. Margaret scored too. Our guards quickly passed the ball to the middle of the court and over to the forwards.

"Klein is open," I yelled. Doyle stopped and fired the ball to Klein, who was waiting under the bas-ket. She dribbled once, then laid the ball against the backboard square. Another two points for us. We all clapped and cheered.

The game continued like this for the whole first quarter. Every time we got two points, the other team scored and tied it up. When the buzzer rang, we were just two points ahead.

We formed a circle around the coach. He drew different plays on the board, circled things, and drew lines from one to another. Soon the board was filled with circles and lines, circles and lines. It would have been confusing but I knew his favorite play was the "Give and go."

"As soon as you pass the ball, go towards the basket. Whoever gets the ball, pass it back immediately. Okay, get back in there and keep on doing what you're doing," Coach Brennan said.

The girls ran out to the court, took up their positions, and the second quarter started. It seemed like every time St. Margaret missed a shot, they got the rebound and worked it for a basket. We seesawed back and forth and by the time half-time came I felt completely worn out from yelling and screaming. The score was St. Anastasia, 32 and St. Margaret, 32. Tied up.

We went into the locker room during half-time and sat on the benches. The coach gave us exactly two minutes to relax, then he was all business. "Okay, girls, listen up. I'm proud of the way you're hanging in there and not giving an inch. We're evenly matched," Coach Brennan said. He paced back and forth, back and forth. "This is what we're going to do.

We have to change the momentum of the game. That means we can't let them score every time we score."

Coach Brennan ran his hands through his black hair two times. "What we have to do is steal the ball away from them after we score. We won't let the ball get across the middle. We can beat them with our speed. I'm taking Gustafson out and putting McGiver in."

I was all ears now. There was a collective shocked silence with me being the most shocked of all. I felt the eyes of the whole team on me. "Gustafson is doing good, Coach," I said.

"This has nothing to do with whether Gustafson is playing well. What this has to do with is the fact that you're the fastest one on the team. You had more steals for the time you played than anyone. So, your job is to steal the ball away from St. Margaret's and then pass to Doyle or Klein. And it has to be quick. Grab the ball and pass." He bent down like he was grabbing the imaginary ball from me. As soon as he got the imaginary ball, he made an imaginary pass. "Got it?"

"Got it. But what if I can't steal any?" I couldn't believe it. He was putting his trust in a sixth grader. What if I let my team down? What if I lost the game for us? I would have to leave the court in disgrace and I probably wouldn't even feel like playing next year.

"McGiver, are you with me?"

"I'm with you, Coach."

"Good. Get out there and steal to your heart's content."

We ran back onto the court, took a few practice shots, and when the buzzer sounded, we hurried to our seats. Instead of sitting down, I ran out to the center of the court and took my position for the jump ball. I looked up in the stands long enough to see my dad and Aunt Florence clapping and yelling.

Doyle tipped the ball to Klein and she dribbled towards the basket. After quick passing back and forth, we scored. It was 34 to 32.

Now it was my chance. Instead of guarding my person, I waited halfway on our side of the court.

St. Margaret passed the ball from under our basket. The girl dribbled her three dribbles, stopped, pivoted, and quickly passed off to her teammate. My specialty was batting the ball away when the person dribbled. I zeroed in on where the ball was. My hand went out to knock the ball away and I got only air. I tried again. This time I got lucky. When my hand darted out I caught a small piece of the ball. It was enough to interrupt her concentration and the ball squirted away. St. Margaret grabbed the ball back and threw it over to the other side. I was disappointed but I knew I had my timing down.

The ball came back to us in no time since St. Margaret scored right away. As soon as I got the ball, I dribbled and passed to Klein who decided to set and shoot. The shot was off and St. Margaret rebounded. Well, I dashed across the court and with one move batted the ball away from their girl. Doyle grabbed the loose ball and scored.

St. Margaret got the ball again and I went into action. I was determined to get the ball back and not let it cross the middle line. I chased the first girl who passed to her teammate. I grabbed the ball from the second girl. I heaved the ball to Klein who sped towards the basket. She made an easy lay-up. It was 38 to 34.

I got into a rhythm in that game. I didn't get the ball back for us every time but I did it enough to throw their game off. I hadn't taken a shot the whole third quarter because that wasn't my job. A missed shot ricocheted off the backboard and landed right in my stomach. I automatically did a hook shot and the ball went in. The buzzer rang signaling the end of the third quarter. The score was 44 to 38 with us still ahead.

The coach asked the team if we should play everyone or if we should stick with what we had been doing. The whole team said to stick with our third quarter strategy. I felt a slap on my shoulder from behind. I turned around. There was Patty Bloomer with the biggest grin on her face I had ever seen. "You're winning the game for us," she said.

The fourth quarter started with a bang. Doyle tipped the ball to Klein and we were off. Klein dribbled three times, passed to me, and I passed right back to her. She did a quick lay-up and scored.

St. Margaret got the ball to their forwards immediately; no fooling around. I didn't even have time to try to steal. They scored too. When it was time for our team to bring the ball back to center court, St. Margaret double teamed anyone who had the ball. It made our girls nervous. Anyway, St. Margaret blocked the ball and got it back. They scored again. The game was a real nail biter as Gramps would say.

"Time-out," Coach Brennan yelled.

Doyle put one hand on top of the other to make a tee. The ref blew his whistle and we ran to the sidelines.

"Okay, girls. St. Margaret is doing to us what we did to them last quarter. We have to get our momentum back."

"Do you want me out, Coach?" I asked.

"No, you're still in. Gustafson, go in for Klein. Henderson, stay. Schmit, Lynch, out. You look tired.

Take a rest. Ryan, go in for Schmit. Olsen, go in for Lynch. Don't let St. Margaret get any easy shots. Make them work for the points."

The buzzer sounded. We ran out onto the court. Henderson had the ball out of bounds down by St. Margaret's basket. Ryan and Olsen ran back and forth at breakneck speed trying to get open. Henderson threw the ball to Ryan, who was immediately fouled. The game was turning ugly.

The ball came down to our end of the court and I had to shoot at the free throw line. I made the one shot. The bad thing about getting just one free throw was that the other team got the ball under the basket and I had only scored one point. I had to get the ball back. St. Margaret passed the ball in quickly and started dribbling toward center court. I was in swift pursuit of the ball but the girl rifled it to their forward.

There was one minute 47 seconds left in the game. I kept glancing up at the scoreboard.

St. Margaret scored again. They didn't seem to be missing many of their shots. It was a one point game.

The coach was on his feet and signaling for another time-out. "Okay, girls. Take a deep breath and drink some water. This is what we are going to do. You know the fast break. We're going to add a wrinkle. It's going to be the guards throwing the ball from the other side."

We were all supposed to run towards the basket as soon as the guards got the ball. Then, after we scored I had to steal the ball back so we could score again. It was as simple as that. I didn't tell the coach that I thought St. Margaret was on to me.

We ran out to the middle of the court. St. Margaret got the ball after the jump. They ran towards their basket lickety-split and before we knew it, they had scored. They were ahead by one.

As soon as our guards got the ball inbounds, the forwards ran towards the basket. Henderson threw with all her might and the ball took a couple of crazy bounces and landed almost in Gustafson's lap. She immediately dribbled towards the basket, shot, and scored. St. Margaret was in a state of shock but it wouldn't last so we had to take advantage. When they threw the ball inbounds, I was ready. I hurled my body at the ball. I seized it, threw it to Gustafson who was waiting, and she scored again. One minute 21 seconds away from victory.

St. Margaret passed quickly to center court. One of their girls ran toward the basket. The ball came flying towards her. She snatched the ball, dribbled, and started to go in for a lay-up. Henderson tried to slap the ball out of the air but instead smacked the girl's arm. The whistle blew. The girl went to the free-throw line. She shot right away without setting and missed. She took her time the second shot, dribbled a couple of times, set, and shot. Swish.

As soon as our girls got the ball in, they threw it down the court. The ball was down by the basket but none of us were there so the ball went out of bounds. St. Margaret got the ball back. I tried my hardest to steal but they were passing too fast. The ball was at their end of the court before I could blink twice. This time Ryan fouled the girl trying to score. She sunk both free throws. The game was tied 51-51.

When Ryan got the ball, she let it sail. I stayed at mid court while Doyle and Gustafson went off towards the basket. The ball flew just past me. I ran after it, grabbed it, and looked for my team. Doyle and Gustafson were trying to get free of the three St. Margaret's guards who were waving their arms crazily. I didn't know what to do. I dribbled my three dribbles and looked again. There were five girls running around by the basket. I had no clear pass and no one was guarding me so I decided to shoot. I arced the ball through the air. It hung suspended for a second as it soared towards the basket. The ball hit the rim, the backboard, and the rim again. Then it dropped to the ground. The stands gave a big sigh.

St. Margaret seized the ball and they were on their way to the other side. Olsen kind of went crazy when the person she was guarding drove toward the basket. She flailed at her, one hand after another, just like a windmill. The ref blew the whistle. St. Margaret had no problem sinking two from the free-throw line. Olsen covered up her face while the girl made her free throws. They were ahead of us by two.

I was the only one near the middle so our guards got the ball to me and I started towards the basket. I wasn't about to do what I did the last time. My three dribbles were up and I looked around. Gustafson came rushing past me with her arms outstretched. I passed her a hard pass in the chest. She hung on to it, darted toward the basket, and tried to shoot the ball when a St. Margaret's girl threw herself at her. Anyway, Gustafson ended up sliding along on the floor. The ref blew his whistle.

We lined up in our places while Gustafson got ready to shoot the free throws. The first one went in. No problem. The second shot spun around and around the rim of the basket. While all of us watched the ball fell to the floor, took a gigantic bounce, and landed in the arms of a St. Margaret's girl. She was off like a shot from a cannon. She threw the ball to her players on the other side. I glanced at the clock. Twenty nine seconds remained.

The coach for St. Margaret yelled, "Hang on to the ball. Stall."

The girls started doing their three dribbles sideways and then passing to each other while staying by the middle of the court. Our poor guards were kept busy trying to get the ball back. It was chaos.

The people in the stands stood and yelled, "TEN." "NINE."

"EIGHT." I felt like running over the center line and stealing the ball.

"SEVEN."

"SIX."

"FIVE." Henderson wrestled the ball away from the girl. The ref called a jump ball. Henderson jumped, tipped it to Ryan, who dribbled toward center court.

"FOUR."

"THREE."

"TWO." Ryan hurled the ball toward the basket.

"ONE." The gong sounded. The ball seemed to be in slow motion and for a second I thought it might have a chance. It bounced short of the basket and went out-of-bounds.

The St. Margaret's bench went nuts. They were jumping up and down, hugging each other and screaming. We stood frozen for a few seconds and then kind of skulked off to the bench. Finally, Coach Brennan broke the silence.

"Girls, get in line and shake St. Margaret's hands. I have to say this was one of the most exciting games I've ever had the pleasure of coaching. I'm proud of all of you."

We shook hands in our line saying, "Good game," to everyone. By the end of the line I was thinking it really was a good game.

"Next year we'll get 'em," Coach Brennan said.

"We will, Coach. We will."

Chapter Thirteen

Gramps Goes Home

It had been three days since the big game. The time had gone quickly since Gramps was getting stronger every day. He had physical therapy twice a day and occupational therapy once a day. The nurses got him up in the chair for meals and even though Gramps still had a bad side, he could stand and pivot on his good leg.

While he sat in the chair, I liked to tell him all about the big game. He wanted me to tell him about how I stole the basketballs, how I made my hook shot, and everything else that he missed. He made me act out my stealing strategy and my hook shot. I crumpled up a paper and tried to sail it through the air over to Gramp's wastebasket. It took me three tries until it landed in the wastebasket. I raised my hands in the air and said, "Ta – Da." Gramps cheered like he would've if he'd been there.

I thought Aunt Florence would be joining in our play-by-play discussion but she said her throat hadn't hurt this much since she had had strep throat when she was a teenager. To tell you the truth, I would have never believed that Aunt Florence would come to my big game and cheer so much and so loudly that three days later she could barely talk.

According to Nurse Maggie, Gramps would be moving to the regular floor in the next couple of days. She followed every pronouncement she made with, "If everything goes well." Then she'd say, "We'll see." She said it so often that I kept getting the idea that maybe things wouldn't be going so well after all. I kept my fingers crossed just in case.

I felt like I lived at the hospital now. In fact, I wanted to be there when school was done for the day because, otherwise, I sat at home thinking about Gramps.

The funny thing was that with all the time I'd been spending at the hospital and all my worrying about Gramps, I hadn't even given a thought to the mysterious Daniel. I wondered if I'd ever find out who he was.

My days took on a certain routine. Get up, go to school, wait for my mom after school, ride to the hospital, sit with Gramps, eat dinner in the cafeteria, sit with Gramps again, go home, call Sally, and then do homework. Sometimes I got some reading done at the hospital if Gramps was sleeping. No one stayed overnight at the hospital anymore because, thankfully, he was out of the woods.

Eight days after Gramp's stroke, my mom and I turned the corner to walk into the ICU and sit in our usual spots. Lo and behold, Gramps was not in his room. Before we could go over to the nurse's station, one of the nurses came over. "Mr. Rossini moved this afternoon," she said. "He's in room 112."

My heart skipped a beat like it did when I was scared but this time it was because I was so happy. My mom thanked all of the nurses for being so good to Gramps and taking such wonderful care of him. Then she said she would always remember them.

We walked into room 112 and there was Gramps, sitting in a chair grinning in his crooked way that I now really liked.

Aunt Florence walked in with her starched uniform and her perfectly placed hat, holding a clipboard. She was working as the supervisor so she had to check up on all the different floors and keep things running smoothly. I had to admit that Aunt Florence had quite a commanding presence in her uniform and all.

The overhead page called for the nursing supervisor. Aunt Florence went over to the telephone and said a couple of words. She wrote down something. I tried to catch a glimpse of what she was writing but she moved the clipboard up against her chest. "I gotta go, Dad," Aunt Florence said. "I'll stop by when I'm done with work."

"Dad, they're talking about you coming home in a few days," my mom said. "If everything goes okay, that is."

"I can't wait," I said.

"I can't either," Gramps said. "I miss my bed."

I wondered how he could come home when he needed so much help. And Aunt Florence said that physical therapy was really important. I had quite a few questions to ask my mom. I decided to wait until we were on the way home so Gramps didn't get confused and worried about his ability to be home.

I didn't have to ask my mom all the questions that I was wondering about because she started talking before we even got to the car. "I'll have to talk to your dad and school but I think I can take off the rest of the year," she said.

"Do you think you can take care of Gramps?"

"I'm going to try. Florence is taking a week off after Gramps comes home to help set things up. Physical therapists will come out to the home every day for a week and then three days a week. We can get a nurse to help Gramps take a bath a couple times a week. Florence will go through all the medications with me so I'm comfortable with that."

"What about getting him into the chair and bed?"

"He can pivot pretty well. The physical therapists here said they would help me feel comfortable with transferring Gramps. We'll have to play it by ear."

"Dad and I can help too. What about the steps, Mom?"

"We're going to set up the sunroom with a bed and dresser until he can go up the stairs."

Gramps left the hospital five days later. My dad decided to leave Gramp's dresser upstairs after moving his double bed and bedside stand to the sunroom. It would be just too crowded, my dad said. Gramps agreed. The big stuffed chair would have had to be moved to make room for the dresser. Gramps said the chair was his favorite place to sit. So it was decided. The loveseat had to go. The big chair stayed. We put a couple of folding chairs against the wall in case anyone wanted to visit with Gramps.

He also had a walker to help him because he still wasn't very steady when he walked. And of course, my mom and dad, Aunt Florence and I would help Gramps get stronger.

Chapter Fourteen

Daniel

Instead of going to the hospital after school, I went home now. It became my favorite time of day because I went to the sunroom, now Gramp's bedroom, as soon as I got home. Sitting in the sunroom with the quiet all around us, Gramps talked and talked.

Aunt Florence had said that after a stroke sometimes the person's emotions got really funny. Not laughable funny but just different than before the stroke. She used a strange word, labile, meaning the emotions were close to the surface.

All week Gramps had been talking. He went back over Ellis Island, Giovanni, and, of course, saying goodbye to his mom. Then he jumped ahead to when my mom and Aunt Florence were little and back to how he met Grandma Rose. There were times when I didn't even know what year we were in. He had been emotional at times, crying over Giovanni's short life, for instance, but other times he was matter-of-fact.

He said things like, "No one said life would be easy," and "You just have to take it as it comes."

Well, anyway, we were talking about all the things we were going to do in the summer such as putting up a new garage, when Gramps started crying. This crying was different than any I had ever seen because even his shoulders slumped and his whole body shook. I thought for a minute he was going to have another stroke.

As the sun warmed me from the outside in, I heard something that I thought would literally knock my socks off. Even though I'd been waiting for this my whole life, when I heard the name Daniel, I didn't even react.

"I can never forgive myself for what I did to Daniel." Gramps didn't even look up.

I didn't move. I didn't know if he was even aware of me being there.

"He was such a good boy. My son. My poor, poor son."

There have been times in my life that I've been shocked like when I found out Aunt Florence had a wicked hook shot. This time shock didn't begin to describe how I felt. It was too mild. In fact, I had no word in my vocabulary that even came close. It didn't matter if I had a word or not because the dam had burst and Gramps couldn't stop talking and weeping. And when I say weeping I mean furrow upon furrow of tears running down his cheeks until it looked like a waterfall. Niagara had nothing on Gramps.

Gramps cleared his throat, wiped his eyes, and blew his nose. "I'm sorry, Colette. I didn't mean to talk about this." He blew his nose again.

"It's okay. I don't mind." I meant it too because I wanted to hear everything about Gramp's life. And I now understood what Aunt Florence meant when she talked about the funny emotions of people with strokes.

"Daniel came to me and showed me his enlistment papers. He had joined the Army." Gramps squeezed his good hand into a fist. "He said he wanted me to be proud of him." Gramps leaned forward. "I told him I *was* proud of him. I tried to convince Daniel to change his mind but he told me his mind was made up."

"How old was he?"

"He was nineteen. Only nineteen. I had to tell Rose that he had enlisted. She screamed when I told her. Then she told me if anything happened to Daniel, she would never forgive me."

"Ohh, Gramps."

"Daniel was a gentle boy who wasn't interested in sports or what I thought boys should be doing. I pushed him to be in sports but he wasn't any good.

He thought I wasn't proud of him." Gramps wiped his eyes and blew his nose.

I didn't know what to say. I was thinking poor Gramps but, of course, I couldn't say that.

"Daniel wanted to be a writer but he had dropped out of college. I told him that he might as well join the Army to become a man and figure out what he wanted to do. I didn't really mean it but I couldn't take my words back." He blew his nose again.

Now I really thought poor Gramps.

"Daniel finished boot camp in six weeks. He had ten days leave before he was stationed for two months of advanced training. It was 1951 and I prayed and prayed he wouldn't be sent to Korea. As soon as he finished the advanced training, Daniel volunteered to go." The tissue Gramps had been holding was now shredded. He stopped talking and stared straight ahead.

"Maybe he really didn't know what he wanted to do and thought being in the Army would help him decide," I said.

"Maybe. Daniel had been in Korea a little more than a month when the two soldiers came to the door. Rose was home alone and she wouldn't open the door. She called me at the store and I came right home.

While waiting for me, Rose had let the soldiers in but she wouldn't talk to them until I got there. We both knew that Daniel was dead."

"How horrible."

"It was. The soldiers told us that Daniel had died with honor. Neither Rose nor I said anything to them. They finally excused themselves. I looked over at Rose. She hadn't made a sound during the whole time the soldiers were there. She had her fists clenched on her lap and the tears were running down her cheeks. I wanted to hold her so much but I thought she blamed me. So, I did something that I've always regretted. I walked out of the room and left poor Rose sitting there all by herself."

"Gramps, it wasn't your fault. Daniel made up his own mind."

Gramps took in some deep breaths that sounded like sighs. He looked out the window for a full minute before he continued. "Rose was too kind to say out loud that she blamed me since I blamed myself. But our relationship changed. For the first time in our marriage there was something neither of us could talk about. It became like a heavy weight around our necks."

I moved my folding chair closer to Gramps. Then

I just took his hand and squeezed it like I used to do when he was in the hospital.

"Daniel gave me this when he came home on leave." Gramps reached into his pocket and pulled out his wallet. "Help me, would you? It's folded up in there."

I looked inside the wallet. In the corner where the paper money goes was a piece of paper. I took it out. "Should I open it?"

Gramps nodded.

The paper had obviously been unfolded many, many times. I opened it. As careful as I was one of the creases ripped a little. I looked at Gramps thinking he might want me to put it back.

"It's okay, Colette. You can open it."

MY POP

I want to take this time to tell you how proud I am to be your son. When I think of how you came over here by yourself and then made a life for all of us, I have nothing but admiration for you. How hard you worked, Pop! And how you persevered! Finishing high school while learning English and then going on to pharmacy school was really amazing. I promise you I will finish college when I come home.

I remember how you used to play catch with me even though I never was any good. You pretended that I could be the next Joe Dimaggio if I worked at it but I knew the truth. More than anything I just liked spending time with you. I remember how you put up the basketball court and the only one who could play was Flo. We sure had fun trying to block her hook shots.

One thing I'll always remember is how sometimes we couldn't wait for you to get home so we'd run up to the store to tell you something that had happened at school. You would stop whatever you were doing and then thank us for coming to see you. From the bottom of my heart, I want to thank you for loving all of us and loving Mom. It made our house a happy home to grow up in. I love you so much.

Daniel

P. S. If I get lonely, I'll just think of you listening to your opera records with your eyes closed. Such joy on your face!

D.

Now I was crying and Gramps put his arm around me. And I couldn't stop so he had to hand me a tissue.

I guess I wasn't in such a big hurry to grow up anymore. Just when you thought things were going great, something happened that turned your life around forever. Like losing your only son. How do adults stand it?

Chapter Fifteen

No More Secrets

After finding out who Daniel was, even though I'd been waiting my whole life, I was so exhausted I didn't even ask my mom about him for two days. Instead I listened to every Beatles song I had while I thought about Gramp's revelation. I found that the Beatles were always good for figuring things out. When Gramps was talking I imagined how parents must feel when they lose a child. Gramps said it was a hole that would never go away. He said to begin with, it's an actual physical hurt like your heart is being ripped out of your chest. After a while, the physical hurt goes away but the hole remains. All of a sudden it occurred to me that my mom and Aunt Florence had lost a brother. They must have a hole inside them too.

I told Sally about my Uncle Daniel. She was surprised to begin with but then she said she wasn't. She said she knew it was something really sad and hurtful since no one talked about it. Then she said she was happy for all of us that the secret had finally come out. We decided we would never have any secrets from each other.

My mom and I were alone in the kitchen two days after the revelation. "Gramps told me about Daniel," I said to my mom. I wondered if Gramps had told her about our conversation.

"I'm glad, Colette. Your dad and I have talked about when we should tell you many times."

"Then why didn't you?"

"Why don't we sit down?" My mom pulled out the chairs around the small kitchen table. We both sat. She started talking quietly at first. "Your dad and I wanted to tell you. We thought you were old enough to hear about it. I guess it was because of Gramps. He couldn't talk about it. We thought we were protecting him."

"Didn't you think I should know that you had a brother and I had an uncle?" I had to admit that I was kind of mad at my mom for not telling me.

"Yes, I thought you should. I apologize for not answering your questions when you tried to find out who Daniel was." My mom buttered a piece of toast and gave it to me.

"Mom, do you miss him?"

"Terribly. Everyday."

After my mom said how much she missed Daniel, I wasn't one bit mad at any of them. "What was he like?"

"I find him very hard to explain to someone who didn't know him," my mom said. "He was one-of-a-kind. He was funny, never mean but he loved to tease. How he loved to tease! Gramp's love of opera was one of his favorite subjects. He'd act out the parts. We'd all laugh as Gramps protested Daniel's lack of appreciation for the finest music in the world." My mom hesitated for a few seconds. Then she continued. "He was intelligent. He loved to discuss poetry and literature with your grandmother. He was one of the most curious people I have ever known. Other than you, that is." My mom smiled at me. "And so handsome. He looked a lot like Gramps did when he was young. He was always there for Florence and me. Florence was devastated when he died."

"Were you devastated too?"

"Yes, I was devastated. But I had your father. Daniel died about two months before we were married. I felt bad leaving Florence to get married but Gramps said the wedding would go on as planned. Your dad had been living in a tiny apartment about a mile from the house. He had taken out another year's lease before Daniel died. That's where we planned to live. Gramps said that we should live where we had planned. So your dad and I married. Florence, my mother, and Gramps lived in the house. My parents were like angry ghosts not talking to each other or to us. Florence was completely lost."

"It must have been awful."

"It was. We tried to have Florence over as much as possible. Did Gramps tell you that he blamed himself?"

"Yes. He said he had told Daniel to join the Army. And he said he was harder on his son than you and Aunt Florence. Why do you think Daniel joined the Army?"

"I don't know. He always talked about all the places he was going to see. He had pictures of things like the Pyramids of Egypt and the Great Wall of China in his room. I suppose he thought this was a first step to getting away from a small town and seeing the world. Who knows? Do you want anything else to eat?"

"No thanks." My mom had been misty-eyed a couple of times as she was talking. Now she was clearing her throat so she probably couldn't talk much more. I didn't want another Niagara Falls like Gramps. I left the kitchen and then I thought of something. I went back and stood in the kitchen door. "I'm sorry you lost your brother. I really am."

"Thanks, Colette. Give me a hug and then on with you."

After dinner, my dad asked if I wanted to go for a walk. I said sure since I planned on asking him about my Uncle Daniel. We were barely out the door when he brought it up. "Gramps told you about Daniel, I heard."

"Yes, he did. I felt so sorry for him; I didn't know what to say."

"You didn't have to say anything. You listened."

"Did you like Daniel?"

"Very much. You couldn't help but like him. He was always laughing and joking around. People got caught up in his enthusiasm. He wanted to see and do everything. He was always talking about seeing the Taj Mahal or the Louvre or the Grand Canyon. He loved life and he really loved people."

"Mom said that Aunt Florence was devastated."

"She was. She talked to Daniel about everything. He used to tell her that she didn't have to be so afraid of boys. After all, he was one and he wouldn't hurt her."

"He was nice."

"He loved his family. Just like I do."

"Was it hard to get married with everybody sad and all?"

"Your mother and I wanted to get married but we didn't know if it was a good time. We offered to postpone the wedding but neither Gramps nor your grandmother would hear of it. They tried to make the day as happy as possible for us. It really was a wonderful day."

"Did Gramps and Grandma Rose talk to each other?"

"For the wedding. I thought that maybe planning the wedding would bring them out of their grief. But after the wedding they went back to their silent prisons. We couldn't do anything about it."

"Mom said Aunt Florence used to come over a lot."

"She needed to get away from the house. She had intended to go to college in the fall but when Daniel died, she was lost."

"She went to nursing school later?" I asked. I had assumed that Aunt Florence went straight to nursing school after high school.

"Yes."

All of a sudden I remembered Aunt Florence talking about the nurse hugging her while she cried. What was that all about? She did say that's why she became a nurse. Where was she when she was hugging that nurse? My mom had never said a word about that conversation. Were there other secrets in the family?

My dad and I continued walking along the sidewalk. It had started to rain a little bit. My dad asked if I wanted to go back but I said I didn't care. It was a soft, spring rain so everything smelled fresh and clean.

My dad's face was very serious. The more my dad talked, the more questions I thought of. It was kind of confusing. "That's just the way it is. Don't you agree, Colette?" My dad stopped walking and looked at me. "That's what family's for. You're there for each other when times get rough."

I linked my arm with my dad's. The clack, clack, clack of our shoes on the wet pavement blended with the pitter patter of the rain.

Chapter Sixteen

Red Wing

Gramps and I had not had a heart-to-heart in about ten days. Physical therapy still came three times a week. The sessions were only 30 to 45 minutes each but they were really intense. Gramps was exhausted on the days of therapy. I just kind of waved to him on those days.

My mom and Aunt Florence helped him with his exercises in the evenings. Gramps was absolutely religious about his exercises. He worked on his legs, his arms, hands, and even fingers. I could tell that his weak side was getting stronger although he still used the walker. His bad leg dragged and his bad arm drooped but all in all he was making progress. They were almost ready to try the stairs so Gramps was happy he'd be able to go up to his room again.

Another thing he was religious about and would never miss was taking his blood pressure pills. That made Aunt Florence ecstatic.

I had finished my paper about Gramps coming over from Italy, going through Ellis Island, living in Chicago, and then ending up in Red Wing. I put pictures of the Statue of Liberty and Ellis Island in my paper. Mrs. Bosworth loved the part about Gramps making the leather mittens and selling them on the street during the Depression. Some of the kid's ancestors had come over from Ireland during the Potato Famine. Others came from Germany, Norway, or Sweden. Our ancestors left their countries for different reasons but the one thing they all had in common was they wanted a better life for their kids and grandkids.

Mrs. Bosworth said one of the things immigrants found in Red Wing was the rich, black soil of Goodhue County. She said it was perfect for growing wheat. Red Wing had been a leading exporter of wheat in the late 1800s. And she said, the immigrants brought skills with them like the immigrants who started Red Wing Pottery and Red Wing Shoes. The immigrants used their ideas to start businesses that became part of our wonderful Main Street. She told the class to go look at the St. James Hotel so we could see the beautiful woodwork and handiwork from 1875.

My class was relieved when our papers were done because we thought the rest of the school year would be a breeze. We should have known better. Mrs. Bosworth believed in tying up what she called loose ends. "What kind of a teacher would I be if I left this for next year's teacher," she would say. "Why, I wouldn't even be worth my salt." So we went along with her because there wasn't much else we could do and she worked us like dogs. We read new books, wrote papers, discussed historical events, and computed equations like our lives depended on it. I wished someone would tell her that the end of the year was supposed to be fun. I started counting the days until summer vacation. I barely had time to talk to Sally. It wasn't fair.

One day I went to the sunroom to see if Gramps was awake. He was. He had an opera record playing something godawful in Italian. I thought of Daniel.

"Are you sure that's really music? Maybe you just want Mrs. O'Neill from church to come over and sing in person."

"I don't think so. Church is all she can handle. You can turn the record off if you want," Gramps said.

I carefully plucked the arm with the needle off the record. Then I put the record back in its jacket.

"So you've been pretty busy in school."

"I have to say that I'm not going to miss Mrs. Bosworth one bit. No, sir. Actually, I'm thinking about not going to college at all. It's just too many years of papers and books, papers and books."

Gramps listened quietly. "Learning isn't always easy," he said, "but it should be exciting when you learn something new."

"You don't know Mrs. Bosworth. She's total drudgery right now."

"Maybe you're kind of worn out from the busy spring and all."

"You're probably right. Maybe that's it. I'm just plain worn out." Then I thought, if I'm this worn out at age eleven and a half, what will I be like when I'm my mom's age? Or Gramp's?

"Summer's almost here."

"I can't wait. Are you feeling better?"

"Much better. One thing about spending time getting better is that you think about your life and the people who have been part of it."

"I hope I've been a good part of your life."

"You've been the best. My favorite grandchild always."

I bowed.

"Colette, I want to tell you more about your Grandma Rose. Are you up for it?"

"Sure, Gramps." Oh good, I thought, another of Gramp's stories.

"I think when we came to Red Wing is where I left off. Does that sound right?"

"She helped you in the store with bookkeeping and at the soda fountain."

"Yes. After Daniel and Florence were born, Rose brought the children to the store with her. They loved working in the soda fountain. When her father, Paddy, visited his favorite thing to do was serve malts and sodas.

"I like doing that too."

"We had both thought that Red Wing would be a great place to raise a family and we were right. Sundays were my favorite days because the store was closed. I had the whole day with Rose and the children. We would walk by the river to watch the paddlewheel boats. Daniel loved the river. We didn't own a car but sometimes I borrowed one from friends. We would drive down to Lake Pepin so we could see the eagles. All the kids clapped when the eagles swooped down towards the water." Gramps made a swooping motion with his right arm. "My favorite thing was to drive south along the river bluffs to Winona. It was so wonderful in the fall. The colors were just so beautiful. Rose and the kids would ooh and aah."

"Were Daniel, Mom, and Aunt Florence close to each other?"

"They were very close. Rose and I were content with the way things had turned out. She thanked me for bringing her to Red Wing. I felt like the luckiest man in the world."

Gramps got up from the armchair. He didn't like to sit too long. He used a cane now instead of his walker so he picked it up and leaned on it. He spoke quietly so I had to bend forward. "I noticed that Rose seemed awfully tired after Daniel died. Sometimes I'd come home from work and Rose would be sleeping on the couch. I didn't know what to do. She was doing the bookwork at home and spending less and less time at the store. I thought it was because of Daniel."

He continued. "Something told me to go home for lunch that afternoon. Rose was on the couch as she had been other days but this was different. I tried to wake her and I couldn't. I called an ambulance right away."

"How scary."

"Yes. Rose had had a stroke caused by a blood clot. As they did more tests they found she had an irregular heartbeat. She eventually went to the Mayo Clinic. They said they could put her on different heart medications but they couldn't do anything about how enlarged her heart was. It wasn't pumping very efficiently. One doctor said what she really needed was a new heart."

"They can do that now, Gramps."

"I know, they can do so much more today. Anyway, she finally came home with oxygen and we set up her bed right here in the sunroom. Every day I talked to Rose about our life together. It was healing for both of us. When we could talk about Daniel, we could also forgive each other. We even laughed about how mad she used to get whenever kids were mean to Daniel."

Gramps said things like, "that's the way life goes," probably because he wanted me to think that these were just things that happened to everyone. Maybe they were but I still felt so sorry for him. "I'm glad you could talk to Grandma Rose," I said.

"I don't know what I would have done if we hadn't had that time. We had been such good friends. And the silence was so cruel. I look at that time now as a great gift."

"What happened next?"

"Excuse me, but I have to sit back down." Gramps shuffled over to the armchair and eased himself down slowly.

"Rose made me promise not to send her back to the hospital. It took me a long time to agree. The doctor said she had congestive heart failure. We had nurses with her night and day. I was glad everyone was here when she died. She looked so peaceful. I liked to think she was with Daniel. I still like to think of them together." Gramps looked over at the table. "Colette, would you bring me my wallet?"

His wallet was on the table. I brought it over to him.

"Look behind my license. It should be there." I found another well-worn piece of paper folded carefully behind his license.

I unfolded the piece of paper and saw the familiar handwriting.

MY MOM

First of all, I want to tell you how lucky I am to be your son. You taught me to love poetry and the written word. We discussed all the foibles of humanity and all the nobility too. When I wrote something you acted as if it were as treasured a piece of writing as Robert Frost or Hemingway. It made me work even harder at it.

You and Pop are the perfect team. I can't imagine one of you without the other. The love and respect you have for each other taught me that people could stay in love for a lifetime. How I loved

Sundays when we'd walk down by the river and then you'd make fried chicken or one of your other famous meals.

My friends were jealous that I got to be with my mom at our family store. You were always so patient as I "helped" you with the customers. How I loved pulling down the soda fizzer over and over again.

I'll always remember you and Grandpa Paddy behind the soda fountain. What a comedy duo! Both of you knew all the kids and their families. How many times did you give a free Coke or soda to a kid who didn't have any money? When I think of you I think of a person so filled with love that everyone around you feels it. I love you so much.

Daniel

P. S. The guys at boot camp are a lot bigger than the kids on the playground. You better start lifting weights.

D.

I was crying again. Gramps had the tissue next to him so he handed me one. I had to blow my nose before I could talk. "I wish I had known both of them," I said.

142

"They were very close to each other. They just loved the same things." Gramps looked out the window as he had so many times while talking.

"I bet they're in heaven together."

"I think so too."

Chapter Seventeen

My Family

The day was beautiful. It was one of those May days when the air was filled with the rich perfume of blooming lilacs. A day like that was full of promise and young love, my mom would say. We had had some rain in the last couple of days so the grass and the leaves were all different shades of green. Against these tints of green, the cornflower blue sky looked clear and endless. Everything was new.

I went into the sunroom after I got home from school and to my surprise Gramps wasn't there. "Hello," I yelled. "Anybody home?"

"We're out here," my mom said.

I walked out in the back yard and there was Gramps sitting in the sun with my mom. "I suppose you're working on your tan," I said.

"The sun feels so good," he said.

"Gramps walked out here," my mom said.

"Wow. I can't believe it."

"Colette, would you mind if I run up to the store for a few minutes? Florence will be home soon."

"Sure, Mom, go ahead. Gramps and I can find plenty to talk about."

My mom left and I sat next to Gramps. "Pretty soon you'll be able to go to the store. The customers have all been asking about you."

"I've missed being there."

"I remember how excited I used to get about going there. I couldn't wait to help at the fountain. I still make a pretty good malt and a great chocolate soda."

"I never heard any complaints so they must have been good. I liked having you around at the store too."

Gramps had promised me that we would look at pictures of Daniel and Grandma Rose and her family. We had two old photo albums but through the years we had never spent much time looking at the photos. Gramps said he would put the pictures of Daniel back in the albums and then we could look at them.

"I have the photo albums next to my bed. Do you mind getting them?"

"Sure, Gramps. I'll go get them."

Gramps opened the albums carefully because they were old and kind of falling apart. Each black and white photo was held in place by little corner brackets. Some of the photos were really little and the people in them were tiny.

"This is my favorite picture of Daniel," Gramps said. He held up a picture of my uncle with his uniform on. "This was the last picture taken of him."

I took the picture from Gramps. It was the first time I had ever seen a picture of my uncle. I stared at my uncle Daniel. His eyes were black like Gramps and mine. And his hair was also shiny and black. My mom had said Daniel looked a lot like Gramps. Even though Gramp's hair was snow-white now, I could see it. Daniel was tall and standing straight as could be. "He looks proud, Gramps."

"He loved wearing his uniform."

We looked at other pictures of Daniel. Gramps called it a journey back in time. Sitting on the front steps of my house were Daniel, my mom, and Aunt Florence. Daniel was in the middle. Another picture showed the three kids standing by the river. Daniel was pointing at a paddlewheeler on the river.

"That was his favorite boat," Gramps said.

There were pictures of Daniel with Grandma Rose and Gramps. Another picture showed an older man holding Daniel up while he pulled down the fizzer to make a phosphate.

"Is that Grandpa Paddy?"

"Yes. Paddy worked at the soda fountain whenever Rose's parents came to Red Wing. He loved having Daniel with him."

Gramps handed me his wedding picture. "Wasn't she beautiful?" Gramps said. Grandma Rose wore a long white dress, white gloves that covered her hands, arms, and elbows, and a veil over her thick, reddish-brown hair. Gramps wore a suit, a vest, and a hat with a brim.

"She was." We looked at other pictures from Gramp's wedding day. He pointed out Paddy and Marie, Grandma Rose's brothers, Liam and Sean, Cousin Beto, and Angella, the woman whom Gramps had rented a room from.

"Whatever happened to all the people from Chicago?" I asked.

"Angella and Beto died right after Daniel's funeral. Beto had been sick for a long time so he couldn't make it to the funeral. Angella came with Paddy and Marie. She was so old and frail. I heard about a month after the funeral that both she and Beto had died."

"Did you go to their funerals?"

"No. I was feeling as sorry for myself as Grandma Rose was. And we were planning your mother's wedding. I should've gone, I suppose. But people seemed to understand."

"And Grandpa Paddy and Grandma Marie?"

"Their hearts were broken when Daniel died. They came to Red Wing for your mother's wedding and then when Rose was sick. After Rose died, they didn't want to come to Red Wing anymore. The town had too many memories. I didn't want to go to Chicago for the same reason. We wrote and called once in awhile but it wasn't the same. I spent all my time at the store after Rose died so I told myself I couldn't leave the business for even a few days. Whenever we wrote, we said that we should get together. It just never quite happened. They died before you were born."

"We still have lots of relatives in Chicago."

"We do. Rose's brothers, Liam and Sean, both married and had five or six children each. We still hear from them at Christmas. And Beto had a huge family. I don't know what happened to all of them."

"Can we go there to see them?"

"I'll have to think about it. It might be hard right now." Gramps pointed to his weak side.

"I didn't mean today. But maybe later in the summer. I'd love it."

"I will think about it. It might be fun. I bet you don't remember going there when you were six."

"I do remember that the buildings were huge and really tall. I'm glad you said you'd think about going for a visit. Promise?" I put my hands in a praying position, then I looked at Gramps. "I don't want to sound all mushy or anything but I've really liked our talks."

"I have too."

I was just going to say something even more mushy to Gramps like I feel like I know you better and I love that when I was saved by Aunt Florence. She came out to the backyard and pulled up a chair.

"Dad, look at you." She put her right thumb up into the air.

"He's trying to get a suntan, I think." When I really looked at Gramps I was still shocked at how white he was. "He walked out here, Aunt Florence."

"That's great. The physical therapy is working."

"Are you going to stay here for awhile? I told Mom I'd wait till she got back."

"Go ahead. I'll stay." Aunt Florence opened the photo albums. "I haven't seen these in years."

"They're really cool pictures," I said. "Don't forget to tell Aunt Florence about the trip we're planning to Chicago."

"When are you going?" Aunt Florence asked.

"Soon. By the end of the summer. Right, Gramps?"

"I said I'd think about it. On with you now," Gramps said.

"Okay. Don't forget."

I called Sally the minute I walked into my room. We talked for a while but to tell you the truth there was so much commotion in the background, I could barely hear her. Between the rat-a-tat-tat and "Oh, you got me" of Joe and Eric and the whining of Anna, my ears were starting to hurt. Sally and I finally gave up and decided we'd talk in the morning.

I pulled out my homework. I had to write a story about an event that had changed my thinking. Mrs. Bosworth said it could be a big sudden event but it didn't have to be. Just something that once it was over, we weren't quite the same.

The only thing I could think of was Gramp's stroke. I hated to dwell on it but it seemed like for the first eleven years of my life not much had happened. At least there was nothing that made me think I was a different person.

Now I could write about the fact that I was so scared I might lose Gramps. I had thought about what he meant to me so many times. I loved our talks. I couldn't think about Gramps without thinking about him leaving Italy, Giovanni, Ellis Island, Chicago, Grandma Rose, and Daniel. I had never thought about any of those things before Gramps told me his stories. Now I couldn't look at him without knowing that there were so many other people inside of him.

I decided I would begin my story with how I thought before. Once I started writing, it was easy. I wrote about how all I ever thought about was the fact that I was the only child in the family. I thought about what it meant for me. Like how I imagined I would have been best friends with my brother or sister; talking into the wee hours of the night and stuff like that. Since Gramp's stroke I thought about how disappointed my parents must have been that they didn't have more children. My mom had even said that when you waited for something as long as they did for me, it was just very precious. And who knows, maybe my brother or sister would be irritating like Sally's. She never talked to Joe and Eric; they were too busy trying to shoot each other. Her older brother John was always busy with his friends so he wasn't around for Sally to talk to either. And Anna, well, that was a whole nother thought. I could have someone going through all my things, spying on me, and then telling on me. The more I thought about having Anna as a sister, the more I wanted to thank my mom and dad for having only me. But then, it could have been little Margaret…

Before Gramp's stroke, I didn't give a thought to what Aunt Florence did as a nurse. I couldn't believe how many things she knew about. I was glad to have

Aunt Florence at the hospital with us explaining what was going on with Gramps. My mom even said she was happy that Aunt Florence and I seemed to be warming up to each other because she loved us both so much.

Ever since I'd learned about Daniel, I felt sorry for everyone in my family. I had wanted so badly to know who Daniel was and it certainly explained some things I had wondered about but now I wished I had known him. I was really sad that I never met him.

How I felt about basketball was never going to change. I thought about it and had talked about it from the time I was little. I would still be talking about it in the future. In fact, I couldn't imagine winter without basketball. One thing I had realized is just how much fun it is to replay the game with people who love to discuss every little play. I had never given a thought to the fact that Aunt Florence had been my age, much less that she loved basketball and had won games with her wicked hook shot. Now, I felt we had something in common. And did she love to talk about every little play. We'd probably be discussing the championship game all summer until I'd be relieved that the new basketball season was here!

I wrote all this down and then I realized that I looked at everyone in my family differently but most of all I was glad they were mine.

Chapter Eighteen

Aunt Florence

My dad had been waiting for the weather to warm up so he could start the new garage. Gramps was so excited that's all he talked about. He had been doing his physical therapy trying to build up his muscles. He had practiced going up and down the stairs with the therapist. My dad said as soon as Gramps could walk upstairs, he'd be able to walk out to the garage. We had the perfect place for him to sit as he handed us nails and screws.

Gramps still used a cane but by the middle of May he could go up and down the stairs by himself. He said now it was time for him to move out of the sunroom and sleep upstairs. My dad said he would move Gramp's bed upstairs; to just say the word. Gramps said, "I'm saying it." So we made a huge deal of moving the bed and other things up to Gramp's upstairs bedroom. I carried the lamp for his bedside table. I set it down on the table and said, "Ta - Da." Gramps said pretty soon he was going to get rid of his cane too. I said we'd all cheer. "Ta - Da."

My dad had gotten a building permit at the beginning of May. He finally decided that the date to start the garage would be over Memorial weekend. He had the Sunday off, of course, and the Monday too so we had two full days to work on the garage. My dad said he had a dilemma. He had to take down the old garage roof and walls first.

Two of our neighbors had said that they would help my dad with the garage if he needed it. Since Gramps was still pretty weak and my dad wouldn't let me do much except pound nails, he needed help, believe me. Otherwise, he said it would probably take the whole summer. He hoped with the neighbors assisting him the whole garage would be done by the Fourth of July.

Sunday morning we had to go to nine o'clock Mass before we started working on the garage. Gramps was really happy to be at church. People were shaking his hand and slapping him on the back. He grinned, with just a little droop now, from ear to ear.

The hour couldn't go by fast enough for me since Mrs. O'Neill was in what my mom would call rare form. It was Memorial Day weekend so she led the congregation in the "Battle Hymn of the Republic" at the end of the Mass. When she sang "Glory, Glory Hallelujah," her leading turned into a screechy solo. I wanted to yell out Hallelujah when it was finally over. I swore my ears would ring for a week.

We skipped breakfast at the diner and went right home. After my mom's bacon and eggs, Dad and I made our way to the garage. I wore the belt my dad had given me to hold nails and my hammer.

The first thing we had to do was take down the roof. My dad told the two neighbors we were starting and they pitched right in. We started on the side that was tumbling down because it wasn't on there as tightly as the others. I had never minded being up on a ladder and there was a time that I used to live up on the roof with a book. Now I was up there ripping off the shingles and just throwing them in the big dumpster my dad had rented.

My dad, the neighbors, and I ripped things apart for two full days. The only thing left standing was the cement floor with all the lumber on top of it. My dad covered the lumber with waterproof tarps and held them down with bricks.

"We make a good team," my dad said.

I bowed.

"Thank you," he said to the neighbors. "Next weekend, I'll need more help."

"Count us in," they said.

"Remember Gramps and I are ready whenever you need us too."

School would be out in a week and I couldn't wait since Mrs. Bosworth was still wracking her brains trying to think of things for us to do. It was hard not to look out the windows of the classroom and think about summer things like swimming, walking by the river, listening to the Beatles on my record player, biking with Sally, tanning with Gramps, and reading my favorite books while listening to the birds sing. Of course, this summer we'd also be putting up our new garage. Anyway, I knew I'd be thinking about all those things while looking right at Mrs. Bosworth so I wouldn't see her sturdy brown shoes planted next to my desk.

Aunt Florence asked me if I'd like to ride with her up to St. Paul the day after school let out. There was a store she loved up there called Dayton's. She said it was expensive but the quality was good. She sure didn't believe in buying cheap clothes. She would say, "The only thing that happens is you end up replacing them sooner than later and it costs you more in the long run."

I said yes because I didn't have anything else to do. Anyway I thought my mom may have some jobs for me to do around the house. I was home for the summer but so was my mom. And she liked to keep me busy. I protested and said I thought it was summer vacation with an emphasis on word vacation. My mom shrugged her shoulders the more I protested and didn't say a word. Well, anyway, I wasn't in the mood for washing windows, scrubbing floors, or folding laundry. So I said yes, not knowing that the way I looked at my family was about to change again.

I liked the drive to St. Paul. The softly rolling hills were so green. Purple, yellow, and red flowers were everywhere. There were farms with fields of corn, soybeans, wheat, and pretty white picket fences. There were lots of black and white cows chewing their cud and horses running through the fields. My favorite part of the drive was when we drove through the city of Hastings. It was about halfway from Red Wing to St. Paul. There were really big, old houses with turrets and interesting designs. Aunt Florence called them Victorian houses. I loved them.

Aunt Florence and I talked about the usual things on the way to St. Paul. It was fine but you can only say so much about new garages, summer plans, and school. Then we got onto basketball and the miles flew by. We went through all the plays of the big game again. By the time St. Margaret made the winning shot, we were in St. Paul. I planned to ask Aunt Florence about her basketball career on the way home.

I actually loved Dayton's too because we had no store like it in Red Wing. There was rack after rack of every kind of dress, pants, and shirt. There were perfumes and makeup and all different kinds of pretty china.

Aunt Florence took me to lunch at the River Room. Everyone was dressed up. Aunt Florence said her favorite meal was Turkey Divan. She told me that I would love their quiche since I liked eggs so much.

I ordered the quiche. We also got a salad and a popover that was out of this world. It literally melted in my mouth along with all the butter I had put on it. I hadn't even finished my popover when the quiche arrived sitting on a piece of lettuce. I bit into my quiche and thought I was in heaven.

I had been so busy eating that I hadn't even noticed that we were eating on china. And the minute my glass of water was halfway empty, it was filled again. There were candles on the tables so it was kind of dark in there but I didn't mind eating my popover and quiche with Aunt Florence by candlelight.

We left the River Room and then took our time looking at the shoes and dresses. Aunt Florence actually tried on a pink dress that looked nice on her. The style was amazing but the color was just okay. I looked through the rack after she went back to the dressing room and found the dress in red. It was in her size and everything. When Aunt Florence came out of the dressing room, she put the pink dress back on the rack.

I said, "Here it is in red. That might look great on you."

"Oh, I couldn't wear a red dress." Aunt Florence actually blushed.

"Why not?"

"Well, because I've never worn a red dress."

"That's not a good reason. At least try it on." I held up the dress.

"I have no idea where I would wear it."

"We can talk about that on the way home. C'mon, try it on."

"I suppose it wouldn't hurt. Just to try it on I mean." She took the dress from me, looked it over, and walked purposefully into the dressing room.

A few minutes later, I looked over at the doorway. There was Aunt Florence standing in the greatest looking red dress I had ever seen. "Wow. I have to say you look wonderful," I said.

Aunt Florence walked out slowly and then to my amazement she spun around. The dress spun with her.

The clerk had been watching and now she came

over. "That just took ten years off of you. It looks like a dress to go dancing in."

"I don't dance much. In fact, I don't dance at all. So I really don't need it." She turned towards the dressing room. "How much is it anyway?"

The clerk looked at the sales tag. "It's $70.00."

"That's way too much. I'm not going to get it."

"Aunt Florence, remember what you told me about why you shop at Dayton's? You said they really have quality things. This is a quality dress, I would say."

"It's not in my budget." She ran her hands down the dress.

"If you stretch out the $70.00 over the next ten years you'll be wearing it, it'll only cost you $7.00 a year. Anyway, look in the mirror."

Aunt Florence stood in front of a three-way mirror. She bent and moved a little from side to side trying to see the back of the dress. The clerk and I didn't say a word. We just let her wrestle with her budget and the idea that she really didn't need the dress. When I saw her smiling and turning more to the side, I knew the budget and need were swiftly going out the window.

"I'm going to get it," Aunt Florence said. "Yes, I'm going to get it."

"You won't regret it," the clerk said.

I had been thinking that maybe I could talk Aunt Florence into looking at some new glasses but now that she just spent $70.00 I didn't think she would be spending a lot more. "I can't wait for them to see it at home."

We had parked in the parking ramp under the store so we just took an elevator to our car. On our way to the car, Aunt Florence was going on and on about how she had wanted to maybe get me a dress or something new and now she had spent way too much.

"I don't care, Aunt Florence," I said. "I don't like wearing dresses. I didn't come with you so you would buy me something. Anyway, I would never be able to describe just how great you look in your red dress."

Aunt Florence's face looked so happy that her eyes were sparkling kind of like the way that the Mississippi shimmers when the sun plays with the water. It was the strangest thing but with sparkling denim blue eyes, her skin took on a rosy glow and she was actually pretty.

I wondered what we would talk about on the way home. Now that I felt more comfortable with Aunt Florence, I planned on asking her questions about growing up in Red Wing. Maybe the subject of Daniel would come up and she would tell me all about the brother she adored.

In no time we were parked in front of a hospital named St. Joseph's. "I always stop here when I come to St. Paul," Aunt Florence said. "It's something I have to do."

It was so quiet right then that I glanced over at Aunt Florence. She had her hands clasped on her lap. She was still as a cat before it pounces. The eyes, which had been shimmering happily a few minutes before were so flooded with water that I knew the tears would be flowing down her cheeks pretty soon. I thought I had had all the emotion I could stand in the last couple of months. But when I looked at Aunt Florence again, it stopped my thoughts cold. I had never seen a person look quite as sad as Aunt Florence did at that moment.

"What's the matter?" I asked.

"This is where I left Daniel." Aunt Florence continued. "I shouldn't have. I shouldn't have left him." She put her face in her hands and her whole body crumpled. If that wasn't weird enough, she started sobbing so hard that her shoulders, upper body, and even her legs shook. Is this what she did every time she came to St. Paul? Sat in front of the hospital and cried?

"I'm sure he understood. That's the way big brothers are. After all…"

Aunt Florence interrupted. "I'm not talking about

162

my brother." She took her face out of her hands and looked directly into my eyes. "I'm talking about my son, Daniel. I named him after my brother."

Well, you could've knocked me over with a feather, as my mom would say. My mouth, which had been slightly open a minute earlier, was now down on my chest. And it stayed there. Wide open. If there had been any flies in the car, they would've flown right in.

"He was so beautiful," she said. "Just so beautiful."

I guess we were sitting in a spot where people were dropped off because a horn tooted behind us. Not very loud but it was a definite toot.

"Oh, we'd better move," Aunt Florence said. She pulled out into the traffic again. She talked about how great the day had been and how she was so glad to have me with her and then she started talking about the weather. The sky was so blue and everything was so green, things were growing well this year since it hadn't been too hot, thankfully. Then there was silence like I was supposed to answer something. I felt so uncomfortable that I just looked out the window and said nothing.

"Colette, do you want to go to the Dairy Queen?" Aunt Florence asked.

"Sure." I wouldn't turn down a free Dairy Queen if my life depended on it.

"Okay. We'll go over the Lake Street Bridge to the Dairy Queen in Minneapolis. Then we'll sit by the river, eat our ice cream, and talk. How's that sound?"

I didn't know how it sounded. I mean, I did want a Dairy Queen and all but I simply didn't know what to say to her. She had just dropped a bombshell and then started talking about the weather. I continued looking out the window.

Aunt Florence drove over this scary, shaky bridge. I thought the bridge had all the shuddering it could handle until a bus started coming across. There wasn't a lamppost, a railing, or a car that was spared shaking while the bus was on the bridge. A person who had been foolishly walking across the bridge was hanging onto a rail for dear life. I tried not to think about the fact that if the bridge broke in two, we would end up in the Mississippi River.

If the bridge bothered Aunt Florence, she sure didn't show it. Now she was talking about how much she loved the Mississippi and even though Lake Pepin was spectacular, this part of the river was really pretty and, if you could believe it, the beginning of the river was in Minnesota too and you could actually walk across it. Aunt Florence had gone to Lake Itasca with her campfire group in ninth grade and had never forgotten it. She told me that I had to go there someday since it was so beautiful and so wonderful. I said I'd like to go there and then we were at the Dairy Queen.

"What would you like?" Aunt Florence asked.

"A cone would be fine."

"It might melt by the time we drive to the place by the river. How about a malt?"

"Really?" I couldn't believe it.

"Really. That's what I'm going to have. A chocolate malt."

"Could I have strawberry?"

"Of course. Strawberry, it is."

Aunt Florence marched up to the window and ordered two malts, strawberry and chocolate. We got back in the car, drove over the rickety bridge again, and then turned onto a street named the River Drive. I would have enjoyed how pretty it was except all I could think about was the fact that Aunt Florence was a mother. She had a son named Daniel.

In no time Aunt Florence parked. "Here's the Monument. Isn't this a nice view? Let's eat our malts before they melt," she said.

The Monument was a simple tall cross. Gray stone benches sat on each side so they made a circle around the cross. Aunt Florence said it was a remembrance to those who had died in World War I. We walked in front of the Monument where we could see the high banks on both sides of the river and the shaky Lake Street Bridge.

"I often come down here when I'm in St. Paul," Aunt Florence said. "I feel at peace here. I told you we would talk, didn't I?"

I nodded.

"I asked your mom if it was okay to tell you about my son, Daniel. She said it was fine with her. I want you to know that. But I suppose the story really begins with my brother, Daniel."

We walked back towards the Monument. Aunt Florence chose a bench. We both sat down. I slurped my malt because it was so good. Aunt Florence didn't seem to mind. "My brother loved the river. Did Gramps tell you that?" Aunt Florence asked.

"Yes. So did my mom."

"Daniel was such a positive personality that when he walked into a room it actually brightened. Everyone who talked to him was talking and laughing within a few minutes. He literally lifted my soul when I was with him." Aunt Florence stared straight ahead for a few seconds.

She continued softly. "I can't describe what it was like after my brother died. I lost my best friend, my protector, the person who could make me laugh. I didn't know what to do without him."

I didn't know if I should look at Aunt Florence or concentrate on my malt. I decided on my malt because it was so good. I gave another slurp.

"We were in the process of planning your parent's wedding when the news came. Gramps and my mother said the wedding had to go on. It was a diversion for all of us because my parents had something to talk about. But it was the only thing they talked about. When the wedding was over, the two of them passed each other silently in the house. It was awful to be at home. I spent as much time as I could with your mom and dad but I had to go home sometimes. I started being away from home more and more.

"I met a man named Roy. He came into the store selling pharmaceutical supplies. He was handsome, charming, and fun. I thought he was wonderful."

Chapter Nineteen

Roy

"You knew that your mom, dad, and I worked at the store?" Aunt Florence asked.

"I knew that."

"Well, about three months after Daniel died, a man came into the store who introduced himself as Roy. He sold pharmaceutical supplies and asked who the owner of the store was. I showed him to the pharmacy where Gramps was. Roy came back to tell me that Gramps was going to buy supplies from him so he would be seeing me every couple of weeks," Aunt Florence said.

"The next time Roy was in town he asked me to join him for dinner. I said no. I thought about it and after I finished work, I walked over to the diner. He saw me through the window and motioned to the chair across from him."

I sipped my malt and didn't move a muscle.

"He was so easy to talk to. I didn't realize how much

I needed to talk. I told him all about Daniel. I told him about my parents and how sad and silent it was at home. I told him about your mom getting married and how much I missed her even though I was so happy for her.

"I told him I simply didn't know what I wanted to do. If I went to college, I had to leave Red Wing and I didn't want to leave my parents. But I didn't want to work at the store my whole life either. Roy assured me I would work it out."

For the first time in my life, I felt sorry for Aunt Florence. She lost the brother she adored. Daniel was her best friend, according to my mom and her. Her parents weren't talking to each other. Her sister got married and moved away. And she had no idea what she wanted to do in her life. How lonely she must have been.

"He listened. When he came into town we would go for long walks down by the river. I told him how much Daniel had loved the river; the sounds of the steamboat's whistles, the eagles swooping down, how the water was always moving and changing. I told Roy how much I missed my brother. He comforted me. I became very dependent on him."

I had finished my strawberry malt. I opened the cover just to make sure it was really all gone. I slurped a little more and then heard Aunt Florence slurp hers.

"Good to the last drop," she said.

"Agreed," I said.

Aunt Florence continued. "I asked your mom how she knew that she was in love with your dad. She said she really didn't know other than she felt happy when she was with him. She said she always wanted to share everything with your dad and she missed him when he was gone. I told her I knew I was in love because that's the way I felt too. Your mom got really worried and started questioning me. She asked me how much I really knew about Roy and what kind of a relationship it could be when the guy came into town for a night or two and then was gone, who knows where, for a couple of weeks. I got angry with her." Aunt Florence looked down at the ground. She took in two deep breaths.

"Your dad took me out one night after I worked at the store. He said that Gemma and he were both worried about me and they didn't want anything bad to happen to me. I said I was eighteen, plenty old enough to make my own decisions. He said, 'Okay, Florence, but you be very careful.' But I wasn't careful. I had never been with a person who made me feel the way Roy did."

Aunt Florence stood up. She took our empty Dairy Queen cups and placed them in a trashcan. She sighed. "Do you want to walk a little bit?"

"Sure." We walked along the sidewalk away from the Monument.

"Am I boring you? All this talk about myself?"

"No, I don't mind." I guess hearing all of Gramp's stories had made me more patient or something because I really didn't mind at all.

"Roy had told me that he lived in Wisconsin and that he was on the road five days a week. That's all I knew about him. I started going to the dances at the St. James Hotel with him."

I thought about Aunt Florence spinning around in her red dress.

"In August, Roy was gone for three and a half weeks. I was so happy to see him when he came to Red Wing that I didn't care what happened. I would tell my parents I was staying overnight at a friend's house and then stay overnight in Roy's hotel room. It was truly crazy. I didn't listen to anyone.

"I had the naive idea that I would be with him forever. I suspected I was pregnant and decided that I would tell him the next time he came into town. I thought we would live in Red Wing, raise a family together, and live happily ever after." Aunt Florence bent down and picked up a rock. She held it in her fist.

She continued. "It was the second week in October. I went to see Roy at the hotel. I couldn't wait to tell him the good news. Before I could tell him, he told me he was married. I was stunned. I asked him if he had children and he said he had two. I ran out of the hotel."

"Did you tell him?"

"No, I never did. All I thought about was how in the world I was going to tell my family."

We had gone quite a distance from the Monument. The sidewalk was on the same side of the street as the river and on the other side of the street were the most beautiful houses. Aunt Florence liked them too. We both decided that we wouldn't mind living in St. Paul if we lived in one of the houses on the River Drive.

"C'mon, let's go this way. It's really pretty," Aunt Florence said, leading the way along a slender path. "It'll bring us right back to the Monument."

Normally I'd be content to just take in the river but I was busting to hear more about Aunt Florence. She must have been ready to bust too because in no time she started talking again.

"I only saw Roy once more after that night. He came in to the store to see Gramps. He tried to talk to me but I walked away."

"How did you tell Gramps and Grandma Rose?"

"Well, I didn't tell them for a long time. I was lost and so ashamed that I didn't know what to do. I kept thinking that they had lost their son and now this. How could I possibly tell my parents how foolish I'd been?

"So, I went to your mother and father. Your dad was so angry that he wanted to find Roy's wife and tell her what was going on. I told him the only place I had ever heard Roy mention was Wisconsin. Your mom just asked what they could do for me. I asked if they would be there when I told our parents."

I had so wanted to know all about everybody and everything in my family. I thought about my mom saying Aunt Florence had had kind of a sad life. And that sad things happened to people. They sure did. Agreed.

"I planned what I would say and how I would say that I was pregnant and I was very sorry to have done this to the family. Then my mother went into the hospital. So that wasn't a good time. We were all relieved that Gramps and my mother were talking again. I didn't want to do anything to change that. I was afraid.

"When my mother came home and was feeling a little stronger, your mom came over and the two of us went into the sunroom which was where we had put my mother's bed and her big oxygen tank."

"Gramps told me that Grandma Rose had a really bad heart. Did she use oxygen all the time?" I asked.

"Yes. She was what they called in those days a 'cardiac invalid.' She was in bed most of the time and she got very short of breath without the oxygen. Someone from, I think, the oxygen company came to change the oxygen tanks every few days. It was hard."

"Poor Grandma Rose."

"We all felt bad for her. And I had to tell her the awful news. I asked for her forgiveness. She had some questions for me about Roy and how far along I was. I told her I was almost four months. Then she hugged me. She asked for my forgiveness for the way she had been after Daniel died." Aunt Florence clenched and unclenched the fist that still held the rock.

"My mother told Gramps the news two days after Christmas. He had very little to say to me except that he couldn't believe I would bring such shame on our family. Two weeks later he told me I would be going to a place in St. Paul until I had the baby. Then I could come back home."

We were back at the Monument again. We looked out again at the river and Aunt Florence threw the rock. I sat on a bench. Aunt Florence sat on the bench next to me.

She continued. "My mother talked to me every day. Mainly she told me that she wished she could turn the clock back to after Daniel died. She said she

174

wouldn't shut people out. It was just too lonely for her and for all of us. She told me over and over how much she loved me."

"She was really nice," I said.

"The best. One day she told me that if she were stronger, she would help me raise the baby. I knew she couldn't but it was so kind of her to say that. Your mom and dad discussed adopting the baby but then decided that it just wouldn't work. I think they were right on that. I would have interfered.

"So in January of 1952 I came up to St. Paul. I had no idea what the next few months would be like."

Chapter Twenty

St. Paul

Aunt Florence continued. I guess I could say she was on a roll.

"Gramps and your dad drove me to St. Paul on a cold Sunday morning. Your mom stayed with our mother since she couldn't be alone. The conversation in the car was quiet. I didn't talk at all. I remember staring out the frosty glaze of the car window at the exposed branches of the trees, thinking how lonely they all looked," Aunt Florence said.

"We arrived at the home I would be staying at about eleven o'clock in the morning. Gramps carried in my small suitcase and asked for the nun he had talked to on the phone. Your dad and I stood off to one side while Gramps and the nun discussed the arrangements. Gramps gave me a quick hug and then he was out the door. He said, 'Take care,' or something like that. Your dad lingered for a minute, gave me a big hug and said, 'It'll be okay. It really will.' He followed Gramps out the door and I was alone."

"Weren't you scared?"

"I was terrified. I didn't know what I would do without my family. I had no friends to talk to. I was totally alone."

"How terrible."

"It was terrible. After a while I made friends there because we were all in the same situation and we all needed to talk. I listened to many stories of love, abuse, sadness and heartbreak. As funny as it sounds, it became a healing time for me.

"I was able to tell the girls about my brother, about Roy, about my mother's illness, and about my guilt. Some of them had lost fathers and mothers; a girl named Maureen had lost both. I felt most sorry for her. She had been living with her sister and wouldn't tell us who the father of her baby was. She was going to live with her brother in Chicago after the baby was born. I still wonder what happened to her."

"Poor girl."

"Oh, she was. She came from a dirt-poor family and she was so sad."

"Did anyone marry the father of their babies?"

"There were some who did. One girl named

Connie talked about running off with the father as soon as the baby was born. Her family hated him and forbade her seeing him. He contacted her whenever he could."

"Did she run away?"

"They ran away to New York as soon as she turned eighteen. I got one letter from her when I was in nursing school."

"Did you write back?"

"No, I didn't. Even though some of the girls were the bravest people I'd ever met, I wanted to put that sad, lonely time of my life behind me. I had the baby in the hospital as I told you. A wonderful nurse let me hold him for a few minutes. I've always been grateful to her. She told me the adoptive parents had agreed to name him Daniel."

I remembered when Aunt Florence got misty-eyed out in the kitchen. She talked about a nurse who hugged her and showed her compassion. "Is that the nurse who made you want to go to nursing school?"

"Yes. After Daniel left the hospital, I had to stay for another three days. The nurse would come in and talk to me. She inspired me.

"Your mom and dad picked me up from the hospital and brought me back to Red Wing. Now it was Gramps and me who were having trouble talking to each other. No one but my mother ever said a word to me about the baby. I suppose they didn't want to upset me but I took it that they wanted to erase the whole thing and pretend that it hadn't happened. I was very bitter," Aunt Florence said.

Sometimes my mom said that things aren't always what they seem. I decided right then and there to write down my mom's sayings in a notebook.

"One day, I told my mother about how kind the nurse was to me, how I would never forget her. My mother asked if I had ever thought about nursing as a career. She said I was plenty intelligent. And science was never hard for me. She got so excited when I told her I would think about it. She said she'd been praying for something to catch my interest and nursing was a career that a person could feel passionate about.

"Well, I wanted to make my mother happy so I did think about it. In fact, the more I thought about it the more I liked the idea. I can still see my mother's face when I told her I was accepted to nursing school in Rochester. She said, 'Bravo, Florence. Good for you.'"

"She was really proud of you, Aunt Florence."

"She was a remarkable person. So loving and so kind. Should we drive home?"

Aunt Florence and I strolled up the path, looked at the river again for a minute, and then walked out to the car. Neither one of us seemed to be in any kind of hurry. We drove away from the Monument.

A few months before I would have never believed that I would actually feel sorry for Aunt Florence, with her being so severe and all. When Aunt Florence talked about all the things that had happened, I understood what my mom meant. It was kind of a sad life. Even though I had made fun of Aunt Florence's lack of boyfriends many times, now I understood that too. She was afraid, afraid of being hurt like that again. So she acted severe.

We were stopped at a red light. Aunt Florence looked over at me. "Thanks for listening to me. I hope I wasn't too hard on you."

"No, actually I enjoyed it." And the funny thing was, I meant it.

All of a sudden I had a wonderful thought. It was so wonderful I couldn't believe it. I had a cousin. I was not the one-and-only grandchild. "I have to say I'm very happy right now." I looked at Aunt Florence as she drove.

"What are you so happy about?"

"I'm not the one-and-only anymore. I have a cousin."

"I guess you do. I hadn't thought of that."

Aunt Florence had a son named Daniel. She

hadn't seen him since he was born. From my math, and I was good at math, Daniel would be eighteen. Maybe finished with high school, maybe a basketball lover, maybe really nice. Anyway, he was all grown up.

I thought and I thought about whether I should bring up the subject since I didn't want Aunt Florence crying like a river again. But I had to know so there was no way around my next question. "Can I ask you a question?"

"Of course."

"You don't have to answer it if you don't want to."

"Go ahead." Aunt Florence glanced over at me. Her eyebrows were raised a bit like a semi circle.

"Well, I was just wondering if you ever wonder where Daniel is. What I mean is, and you can tell me it's none of my business, would you ever like to meet him?"

Aunt Florence's hands gripped the steering wheel. When she answered it was with perfect control. "There hasn't been a day in the last eighteen years that I haven't thought about him. I can't picture what he looks like but I wonder a lot. Did he walk early? Did he like books? Was he scared going to school? Did he love his teachers and did they love him? How old was he when he found out he was adopted? Was he upset? Is he a good student? What's his favorite subject? What kind of music does he like? Does he play basketball or other sports?" Her hands gripped the steering wheel tighter.

"I bet he plays basketball. He'd have to. He's my cousin."

"When you put it that way, I guess I think he loves basketball too."

"Not just loves it but he plays it. And he's got the best jump shot around."

"At least in the family, he does."

"Hook shots. That's different. I bet we can take him on."

"I am a dead eye with a crescent roll." Her giggle let me know that the subject was okay.

"And he listens to the Beatles. I know that for a fact."

Neither of us talked for a couple of miles. I was almost bursting with my next question. "Do you think we could find him, Aunt Florence?"

"What do you mean?"

"I mean if we put all our heads together, I'm sure we can find him."

"I always hoped he would try to find me."

"Maybe he wants to."

"I don't know. What if he doesn't?"

"You won't know unless you try."

"I don't know."

"Doing nothing doesn't find him. We should talk to my mom and dad. I bet they'd help us. They might even have some ideas."

"You know what, Colette?"

"What?"

"You're a very special person. I'm lucky to be your aunt."

"Are we going to search for Daniel?"

"Yes. We're going to search for Daniel."

Chapter Twenty One

A Can of Worms

We had a few surprises for the people at home, Aunt Florence and I. I promised her I would let her bring up finding her son with my mom and dad. And Gramps was just going to have to wait until we had our strategy down.

Everyone was home when we got there. They had all kinds of questions for us about what we did and what we saw. I told them about the popovers, quiche, and the Dairy Queen. My mom, dad, and Gramps each had a story to tell about going over the Lake Street Bridge. Each story got a little better than the last until I became downright amazed that any of us had lived through the experience. All of a sudden I remembered the red dress.

"Aunt Florence, why don't you try on your new red dress for all of us?" I asked.

"I don't want to right now."

"You got a red dress, Florence. Let's see it," my mom exclaimed.

"I'll announce you to the group when you come upstairs," I said.

"Now you're embarrassing me."

"You don't have to be embarrassed in front of your family," my dad said. "C'mon. I want to see it too."

"I do too, Florence," Gramps said. "You must have bought it for a reason. Try it on."

"All right. I got talked into buying it by you all know who." Aunt Florence looked over at me and instead of being mad like I thought she might be, she winked.

"Okay, try it on. We'll be waiting," I said.

She went downstairs to change in her room while we waited in the living room. After a couple of minutes, I decided to wait in the kitchen so I could escort her to the rest of the family. My mom pelted me with questions and wanted me to tell them how she looked. I said, "You'll see. I don't want to wreck it."

I was getting anxious so I whispered quite loudly down the stairs for Aunt Florence to hurry up. She bounced up the stairs looking just as fantastic as she had in Dayton's.

"Are you ready?" I asked.

"I'm ready."

"Okay. Let's go. I can't wait to see their faces." We walked over to the living room and I made my announcement. "Modeling the most fabulous red dress ever made is Dead Eye Florence Rossini. Ta - Da." I stepped aside.

Aunt Florence sashayed into the room. She looked around and then twirled perfectly in a circle. Everyone clapped.

"Oh, Florence, it's beautiful. I love it." My mom had been standing. She went over and hugged her sister. I thought I saw tears in her eyes.

"Florence, my gosh, you're gorgeous," my dad said.

"Quite lovely, Florence," Gramps said. "You'll have to find a place to wear it to."

"I don't think I'm going to wear it outside the house."

"Nonsense. Your mother always said that a good dress shouldn't be wasted hanging in the closet."

"And that's not a good dress. It's a great dress," I said.

"Maybe we should go out for dinner," my mom said.

"Or dancing," my dad said.

"Let's go dancing. We haven't done that for so long."

"Whom would I dance with?" Florence asked.

"With me," my dad said.

"And me," Gramps said. "Let me know what you plan and I'll be there. Colette, you should shop with Florence more often."

"I can't afford it." Aunt Florence laughed.

I bowed slightly. We had a far bigger surprise to tell people but I had made a promise. So we talked about all the places we could travel to with Aunt Florence in her red dress. I suggested New York and Broadway and then pretty soon we were flying off to London and Paris. The funny thing was that the whole time we were deciding which place we wanted to visit first, Aunt Florence sat there just as pretty as you please in her red dress.

A couple months before we didn't even know if Gramps was going to pull through and now we talking about soaring off to all different places around the world. "My vote is London. Let's go," I said.

None of us wanted to leave the living room but finally Gramps said he had to go to bed. Aunt Florence remembered she had to work in the morning so she left right after Gramps. I was dying to ask my mom and dad about when Aunt Florence was in St. Paul but of course I couldn't. And I was dying to ask my mom about the second secret Daniel in our family but I couldn't do that either.

The next day I called Sally in the morning and told her we had to get together. She said after lunch would be great. I rode my bike over to her house and Sally met me at the door. We went right up to her room, checked the closet for stray ears, and then plopped on the bed.

The words tumbled out of my mouth. I told her about eating popovers at Dayton's and buying the red dress. She thought that was really cool. Then I told her about sitting in front of St. Joseph's Hospital while Aunt Florence cried. She couldn't believe it to begin with and then she said, "Hmm, it's all starting to make sense." I told her about driving over the Lake Street Bridge to get a Dairy Queen and then sitting by the Monument while Aunt Florence opened up her broken heart. She said, "Poor Aunt Florence. She was just hurt, that was all." When I told her we were going to try to find Daniel, she got really excited. So I told her that the rest of my family didn't know our plans yet and she said she wouldn't tell anyone.

Mrs. Reynolds yelled upstairs for Sally to come down. She came back to her bedroom in about two minutes. "My mom needs me to baby-sit while she goes grocery shopping. You can stay but we have to be downstairs," she said. It bugged her no end that her older brother John never had to babysit. She said she told her mom it was John's turn but her mom said he was busy and not home. Sally told me it wasn't fair.

"Don't worry. I'll help you," I said.

I hadn't helped her with the younger kids for a while so I had forgotten. I stuck it out for the hour Mrs. Reynolds was gone even though Sally told me I could leave anytime. We had no more chance to talk. Between Joe and Eric's loud dueling and poking each other and Anna's complaining about the unfairness of summer weather since they had no air conditioning, I started getting a headache. Margaret came over with a book. The two of us sat while I read *"The Three Billy Goats Gruff"* to her and pretty soon we didn't even hear the two boys, Anna, or Sally yelling at them all to be quiet.

Saturday night Aunt Florence broke the news to my mom that she wanted to find her son. She told her that I knew the story and wanted to help her find Daniel. I was glad I had kept my promise to Aunt Florence and not let on to anybody but Sally what we had talked about in St. Paul.

"I'll help you too, Florence," my mom said. "I've wondered about him so many times."

"I asked a nurse at work who was adopted if she was curious about her natural parents. She said yes she was and she had met her mother but not her father. She said it was uncomfortable to begin with but her adoptive parents were very supportive."

"How did she find her mother?" my mom asked.

"She found the adoption agency and contacted them. The adoption agency then contacted the mother and the two of them met in a neutral place."

"That doesn't seem that hard," I said.

"You have to go through the agency. If either child or parent isn't interested then it doesn't happen. In fact, the nurse said she knew adults who had been adopted as children who had no curiosity about their natural parents."

"Everyone's different," my mom said. "The emotions must be overwhelming for some."

"You said this nurse met her mother?" I asked. "Does she still see her."

"Yes, she still sees her. The families have met and it's been a positive experience for them. But she said sometimes people have unrealistic expectations. So I'm trying to figure out exactly what my expectations are. And what if he doesn't want to meet me?"

"Florence, you made the best decision you could have made at the time." My mom walked over to Aunt Florence and put her arm around her shoulder.

"I thought I did. But I didn't really have a choice. What if he felt like I abandoned him?"

"Remember what it was like back then. We had lost our brother. Our mother was an invalid. Our dad was grieving first for our brother and then for our mother. It was 1952. There were very few resources for women."

"I had no way of supporting him."

"No, you didn't. You made the best choice for him. I admire that."

"I'm just saying that maybe it's better if I don't stir up a can of worms." Aunt Florence paced over to the window. She tapped her fingers on the windowsill.

"John and I are with you no matter what you decide. But you'll never know unless you try."

"I'm afraid it won't turn out."

"Of course, you're afraid. But doing nothing produces nothing."

My mom was always one for trying things, that was for sure. I was waiting for her to say to Aunt Florence, "What have you got to lose?" which was one of her favorite sayings to me. I almost said it myself but then I realized that Aunt Florence had a lot to lose. She had carried with her an idea of who Daniel was and maybe that wasn't even true. Maybe he wasn't a wonderful basketball player after all.

Chapter Twenty Two

The Letter

It had been a week and a half since Aunt Florence told us she needed time to think. It was hard not to ask her if she was at least leaning one way or the other.

Since it was Saturday, my mom and I were sitting in the kitchen finishing up one of her great breakfasts. "What do you think Aunt Florence is going to decide?" I asked.

"I don't know."

"It's taking so long."

"She's wrestling with herself since she's made a good life. She doesn't want to upset the apple cart."

I guess that was the same as opening a can of worms.

"You know, Gramps has never talked about his grandson," my mom said.

"I hope there aren't more family secrets because my heart can't deal with any more shocks." I put my hand over my chest. "It might just stop beating altogether," I said.

"You're really cute when you say things like that." My mom laughed.

"Aunt Florence said she thinks about Daniel every day. Do you think Gramps thinks about him?"

"Of course. I do too."

"Aunt Florence told me you thought about adopting him."

"Just for a short time. It wouldn't have worked. We both knew that. I think if our mother had been healthier, she would have helped Florence until she got on her feet."

"When did your mother die?"

"Shortly after Florence started nursing school. Mother had been getting weaker and weaker. Even though we had nurses with her 24 hours a day, your dad and I took turns staying overnight the last couple of weeks. It was exhausting."

"Sounds like it." I remembered how tiring it was when Gramps was in the hospital. My mom, Aunt Florence, and my dad only had to stay overnight for the first week. And then Gramps was home in less than two weeks. Grandma's Rose's illness went on for almost a year and a half so I'm sure they were all worn out.

"Mother had more and more trouble breathing. I thought we should bring her into the hospital but

Gramps said he had promised her that she wouldn't go into the hospital again. The doctor came to our house. He said she was in congestive heart failure and there was nothing else he could do. She slipped into a coma. We called Florence in Rochester and she came home right away. Our mother died on October 21st, 1952."

"What did Gramps do?"

"He was lost again but my mother and him had had time to talk about losing their son. Since they forgave each other, it wasn't a bitter type of sadness. He was happy that the two of them had time with each other."

"Gramps told me about taking care of Grandma Rose when she was sick. He said it was a gift to be able to talk to her."

"Yes. We were all happy for them even though our mother was so sick."

"Do you miss her?"

"Every day. Every single day."

I wondered if I was just going to be missing people left and right as I got older. I got kind of scared because the people I would be missing every single day, I couldn't imagine not being here. It was an impossibility.

"Gramps lived alone in the house and it was so hard for him," my mom said. "Your dad fixed things constantly over here. One day he said as a joke, 'We might as well live here.' Gramps agreed. The subject kept coming up and the rest is history. When our apartment lease was up we moved back into the house. After Florence finished nursing school, she moved home again too."

"Why didn't you or Aunt Florence move away?" I asked the question because I was curious not because I wanted to move to a different place. I was fine right where I was.

"I don't know. We didn't have to worry about Gramps as long as we were here. The four of us got along well. I guess there never was the perfect time to move out."

"I'm glad."

"Do you wish we had our own house?"

"No, I like it just the way it is."

Aunt Florence finally told us that she did want to find her son. She said she had written a letter saying that she would like to meet him if he was interested. All she had to do was send it to the adoption agency and they would take it from there. She said she had already rewritten the letter and she probably would again.

"I guess the plan is to find out which adoption

agency they went through," my mom said. "That shouldn't be too hard."

"I don't remember if they told me. I had to sign papers but I don't remember anything else."

"Let's see. We could contact the hospital first. If we don't get information from them we could contact the home you stayed in. There can't be that many adoption agencies in St. Paul. I'm sure they'll tell you what to do."

"Let's get started, Aunt Florence. There's no time like the present," I said.

"Okay. Let's do it."

"I'll make some phone calls tomorrow and we can go from there," my mom said.

"Thank you, both of you. You don't how much it means to me."

The next day my mom was on the phone all day. She called the hospital and kept getting different numbers to call. I didn't mind at all because she was so busy that she had forgotten about all the jobs I was supposed to do. I turned on the Beatles in my bedroom and lay on my bed singing away. There was no knock on my door because my mom was just too busy making phone calls.

She finally found a woman in the volunteer office

who said she was almost as old as the hospital. She had been there in the early fifties and she remembered girls giving their babies up for adoption. She told mom one adoption agency and then said, "Oh, maybe it wasn't that one. Maybe it was this one." My mom listened for a long time while the woman went back and forth about the names of the agencies. My mom just said, "Mmm hmm," and "I see." Finally she said, "Maybe I should have the names of both agencies."

She called the first adoption agency who said they wouldn't give any information from their records. The woman there suggested that Aunt Florence call herself and then make an appointment with the director. My mom said thank you very much to the woman and hung up.

She then called the second adoption agency and got the same directions but from a different lady. My mom said that that must be the policy of the adoption agencies. She walked around the kitchen, stretched, and said, "Now it's up to Florence. I can't do any more."

My mom told Aunt Florence what she had found out as soon as she got home. I guess Aunt Florence was one of those people who once she made up her mind there was no stopping her. She made an appointment for the next day in St. Paul at both agencies. She then called her work to say she wouldn't be in. Aunt Florence asked my mom if she would read the letter she wrote to her son after she finished.

Gramps wondered if Aunt Florence was okay when she didn't come upstairs for dinner. My mom said maybe she was tired. After the rest of us finished eating, my mom brought a plate of food downstairs to Aunt Florence. I washed the dishes and had them drying in the dishrack. My mom hadn't emerged yet from the basement. I was dying to know what they talked about but then I thought I better keep Gramps occupied. I watched a guy named Walter Cronkite, whom Gramps loved, give the world news. I said, "Isn't there any good news?" but Gramps wasn't listening to me. I was glad when it was over because I was worn out but then we had to watch the local news. My mom was back in the kitchen by the time the weather was over.

My mom didn't say anything about the letter until the next morning. Aunt Florence's appointment was 9:00 am so she was out the door by 7:30 am. I was still sleeping, believe me. My mom said she told Aunt Florence good luck from me too. She said the letter was so beautiful that she couldn't imagine Daniel not responding.

Aunt Florence got home late in the afternoon.

"How'd it go," my mom asked.

"The first agency had no record of Daniel. The woman listened to me and asked me some questions. She looked through their files and didn't see anything. I told her I also had an appointment at the other agency. The woman said she hoped I had better luck there. So I left and went to the second agency. The woman there said the exact same thing. I hung onto my letter thinking that I shouldn't have gotten my hopes up. So here I am."

"Florence, I'm sorry," my mom said. "What can I do?"

"Nothing. That takes care of it. I may as well throw out this letter." Aunt Florence took the letter out of her purse and started walking toward the wastebasket. "It's okay. It really is."

"So you're just going to give up?" I asked. "I can't believe it."

Aunt Florence stopped walking. "What do you mean? There's nothing else I can do."

"Maybe there's another agency. Are you sure there were only two?"

My mom had been really quiet. She piped up, "That's what the woman in the hospital said. She's the one I got the information from."

"Maybe there was a smaller agency that the hospital didn't use very often or something like that."

"I suppose I could call her back again tomorrow. That wouldn't hurt."

"Don't worry about it, Gemma," Aunt Florence said. "You've done enough. It's just not going to work out."

"I'll give it a try," my mom said. "Maybe there's something that the woman didn't remember."

The next morning my mom got out her paper that had the name of the woman she had talked to and some phone numbers. She sat down with the phone in front of her, looking very serious. I gave the paper a little glance as I walked by. I hoped the lady, the one older than dirt, would talk my mom's ear off like she had the last time.

My mom would be on the phone all day. It would be great. I'd be in my room, listening to the Beatles and thanking God, as I had many times during summer vacation, that Mrs. Bosworth was out of my life forever.

Anyway, the phone rang just as I started walking up the stairs on the way to my room. Evidently the person calling wanted Aunt Florence. My mom got really excited and then she said, "I will tell her that. Thank you so much."

"I'm going to the hospital to see Florence," my mom said.

"What happened?" I asked.

"That was the first agency Florence went to. The woman said that she had found the information on Daniel. She went through every adoption file from 1952 again and it was stuck in the back of one of the other files. She asked if I would give the message to Florence and tell her she'll be waiting for her call."

"Wow."

My mom ran out the front door and I started walking up the stairs again. I heard the door open again and my mom yelled to me, "Get ready to wash windows today, Colette. We've both been kind of lazy this summer."

My hopes for a wonderful day vanished just like someone popped a balloon with a pin. Here one minute, gone the next. Anyway, I couldn't voice my protests because my mom was already out the door. Maybe by the end of the summer I'd be calling up Mrs. Bosworth to ask her to please save me from my mom's summer jobs.

Aunt Florence went back up to St. Paul the next day to meet with the woman from the first agency. She was home by noon.

"I answered lots of questions and then gave the

woman my letter," Aunt Florence said. "She said the agency would relay the letter to Daniel. Then, she said it was up to him. She said as gently as she could that sometimes there was no response. It just doesn't work out. I told her I was trying to be prepared for that."

"All we can do is wait now," my mom said.

"I'm going to keep my fingers crossed," I said.

Chapter Twenty Three

The New Garage

The weeks went by, slowly at first, as we waited for a phone call or letter from Daniel. I stopped checking the mail every hour after three days because I didn't have time for anything else. Pretty soon, it wasn't that we forgot, but life goes on as my mom says.

We worked on the garage all day on Sundays and evenings during the week. I watched Gramps and my dad measure and mark countless times only to measure and mark again. My dad said we had to be sure that everything was in the right place or the garage would be leaning worse than before. Then we would have to start over. They discussed something called codes. I knew we had a building permit but I guess the codes were just as important. Gramps said without them maybe buildings wouldn't be as strong as they should be. I said, "Couldn't we just use more nails?"

My dad had been thrilled that the foundation or slab was "sound and even." He had walked all around it checking with this thing called a level. It had a little tube in the middle that had liquid in it. If it was perfectly level, then an air bubble fit between two lines.

So I waited.

"Antonio, let's get started," my dad said. "I can't think of anything else to do."

Thank God, I thought.

"I'm ready," Gramps said. He still wasn't as strong on his bad side but he could measure, mark, and hold some things up.

My dad showed me the anchor bolts on the foundation. Something called sill plates were to be anchored onto the foundation with these bolts. My dad got the 2x4's from the lumber pile for the sill plates.

"Looks good, John," Gramps said.

In no time the sill plates were down. They looked straight to me but my dad used his level every few inches. Every once in a while he pounded on the sills with his hammer. He gave the nod to Gramps who sprang into action.

Gramps had been hugging his measuring tape. He took his marking pen out of his pocket and walked around the whole garage. The measuring tape came out for a distance and then snapped back when Gramps pushed the button. My dad was busy with his measuring tape too. He lined up what he called studs, the pre-cut vertical boards. Every sixteen inches Gramps put down a mark.

My dad went to get the two neighbors because he thought it would be much too heavy for Gramps to try to hold up the sides.

I couldn't talk about what I wanted to talk about, which was Aunt Florence giving a baby up for adoption. Every day I thought of a new question. How often did they see Aunt Florence when she was in St. Paul? Or didn't they see her at all? I'm sure between the store and Grandma Rose's illness, Gramps had all he could handle. I wondered if he wrote to her. I had to ask my mom about it.

Of course, the thing on my mind now was waiting for the letter. And I couldn't say anything about that. It hung over me like a cloud.

My dad and the neighbors were working like their lives depended on it and they didn't seem to notice Gramps and me after a few minutes. They didn't even need me for hammering nails. They didn't need Gramps with his measuring tape because the places where the studs were supposed to go were already marked.

So Gramps and I had some time for visiting. I

asked Gramps why he hadn't gone back to Italy for the last 25 years.

"When I first came over, I planned to be here a few years and then go back to Italy. If I had known I was never going to see my parents again, I probably wouldn't have come to America. As I told you, I didn't have enough money for a long, long time. Then came the Depression, the Second World War, and both my parents died. I went to Italy after the War but it was just too sad," Gramps said.

"My sister Sofia and I swore that we wouldn't let more than five years go by before we saw each other again. I never wanted to close the store for two weeks so I always thought it would be the next summer or the next summer. After Daniel died, my sister came here."

"You still write to her, don't you?"

"Yes, but I should more often."

"I've got an idea, Gramps. Why don't we go to Italy? As a family, I mean."

"You've got big ideas, don't you?"

"I don't mean this minute. I mean, well, maybe next summer. Next summer, Gramps. You don't have to worry about the store anymore. I want to meet your sister and her family. I want to see where you were born."

"I don't know."

"C'mon, Gramps. It'll be wonderful."

"Maybe we could go next summer. My sister and her family would love it."

"Say no more. Let's shake on it." We shook hands as a promise, something that neither one could go back on. I'd be crossing my fingers until next summer if I had to.

"Wait a minute. What about Chicago? I thought you wanted to go there."

"I do but we can go there anytime. Next summer, it's Italy."

My dad signaled he was ready for Gramps and I to pound nails. I pounded in the nails a little bit first for Gramps because he couldn't hold the nails with his weak side and hammer at the same time. I set up several for him and then I started hammering in my area. Gramps and I hammered nails into the bottom of the walls that lay on top of the sill plates. It was really fun. The corners had three studs each and were tied together. The garage was filled with the banging and clanging of hammers hitting nails. My dad said, "This is a time when you can get really aggressive." The corners were nailed together and we had the frame of the garage.

Before we went back to the house, I made Gramps

shake my hand again. "You know what the promise is, Gramps."

"I remember."

My dad bought something called trusses for the roof. They were premade and looked like triangles. He said they were really heavy so the neighbors would be back on the weekend.

The two neighbors were there bright and early on Saturday morning. My dad had taken the day off from the store since one of the neighbors couldn't come on Sunday. He actually had to close it for the whole weekend. He said you just had to take the help whenever you could get it.

Gramps and I found the perfect perch to watch the trusses go up. There was a little hill at the back of the house where we could see everything my dad and the neighbors were doing. We settled right into our two folding chairs.

"Colette, what do you want to be when you grow up?"

"With all the listening to secrets I've been doing recently, I should probably be a psychiatrist," I said.

"Maybe the family should get a couch for your room and then everybody can take turns."

"Do you want to be first?" I asked. Gramps still didn't know what Aunt Florence had told me in St. Paul so I had to close my mouth just in case something slipped out about the second Daniel.

My mom brought the two of us cold lemonade. Then I helped her bring some to my dad and the two neighbors. We exclaimed over how quickly the garage was taking shape.

After the trusses were secured, my dad signaled Gramps and I. "I was just getting comfortable sipping our lemonade, watching the garage go up," I said to Gramps.

"Maybe we should take the rest of the day off." Gramps laughed.

"We've been working way too hard."

My dad showed me how to nail the plywood onto the outside walls. He cut the sheets with a saw and then Gramps held the sheets up while I pounded nails. My mom came out to help us too. When Aunt Florence came home from work, she grabbed a hammer too. Aunt Florence and I were the nailers and Gramps and my mom were the holders.

"Anyone want to break for dinner?" my mom asked.

"I'm having too much fun," Aunt Florence said. She took aim at the nailhead with her hammer, gave it a swift whack, grabbed another nail, and did the same. "Voila," she said.

"Aunt Florence, what other talents do you have? I asked.

"You never know." She sunk another nail.

My dad wanted to put the plywood over the trusses too but my mom said we needed to eat since it was already 6:30 pm. They talked back and forth until Aunt Florence said, "I'll go to the A & W for everybody. But let's finish as much as we can."

I couldn't believe my luck. A & W had the greatest root beer in the world and their burgers and fries were great too. "I'm game," I said. "We're almost done with the walls. We can finish the roof too."

Aunt Florence even climbed the ladder to help my dad on the roof. Gramps yelled, "You're amazing."

It was 8:15 pm before we finished. "Thank you, everybody," my dad said. "We should do this more often."

Aunt Florence asked me if I wanted to help her bring the A & W home. I said, "Sure. I'd love to."

My mom decided that since it was still light we should eat outside while admiring our new garage. So that's what we did. We sat outside in the full bloom of Minnesota summer while we ate hamburgers, french fries, and sipped root beer from the A & W. After each crunch of a french fry and slurp of root beer, someone made a comment about our wonderful new garage. By the time the brilliant reds and pinks of the sunset had faded, the mosquitoes were biting with a vengeance, so we went inside the house.

Over the next two weeks, we nailed shingles onto the roof and siding onto the outside walls. I mostly handed the shingles to my dad and he nailed them into place. With the siding, sometimes I got to nail the pieces and so did Gramps. My dad was happy because we had finished before the Fourth of July. It was time for my dad to park his car in the garage. The whole family stood next to the garage to cheer my dad on. Ta - Da! Aunt Florence always parked her car in the front of our house but now she said she'd reserve a space for the winter.

"Look what we can do when we work together," my dad exclaimed. 'I'll let you all know what my next project is."

"I'll be there, Dad," I said.

Chapter Twenty Four

The Reply

It was almost a month before Aunt Florence got the letter. It had gone to the agency first and then been sent to Aunt Florence. She took it downstairs so she could be alone. When she came up for dinner, she said nothing. I thought that the news must be bad. Maybe her son had said he wasn't interested. As I watched Aunt Florence, she didn't seem upset. She ate like she normally did, but almost with a light-heartedness. I thought the news might be good.

"I have an announcement to make," Aunt Florence said.

I crossed my fingers.

"I got a letter from my son today."

"What?" Gramps stopped eating.

"Yes, Dad, I wrote to my son a month ago. He wants to meet with me." She leaned forward in her chair.

"I'm so happy for you, Florence," my mom said.

"I can't believe it." Gramps said. "I'm speechless."

"I can't believe it either," Aunt Florence said. "I didn't know if he would want to meet me."

"Can't we meet him too?" I said. "I'll be really mad if I don't meet him. Since it was my idea and all."

"What do you mean it was your idea?" Gramps asked. He still had not taken a bite of his food.

"It was my idea, Gramps. Just what I said."

"So you knew about this. And didn't tell me." Gramps looked around the table. "You mean everybody knew about this but me?"

"Dad, I didn't want you told," Aunt Florence said. "I was afraid that I wouldn't hear from him and you'd be disappointed. Please don't be mad."

"What do you have to do, Florence?" my dad asked.

"I have to call him about where we should meet. Depending on how that goes, he may decide not to see me again. It's his choice."

Gramps wasn't saying anything. I wondered if he was feeling bad that we had all been keeping a secret from him.

Aunt Florence showed the letter to us after the dishes were done.

Dear Florence, (I hope you don't mind me calling you that)

I was surprised to get your letter. I read it twice the first day I got it. Then I put it aside for a couple of weeks and read it again.

I had to think about what I wanted to do and what I wanted to say to you. The first thing I had to do was talk to my parents and make sure whatever I decided was all right with them. My mother wasn't sure that it was a good idea to meet you. She didn't want me to be hurt, she said. I told her I wouldn't write to you until she said it was okay with her. My dad thought it was okay from the beginning. He must have talked it over with my mother because she changed her mind. They both gave me their blessing to do whatever I felt was right.

Thank you for thinking about me through the years. To answer your question, I found out I was adopted when I was eight. I spent a lot of time for a couple of years wondering about you and the reasons for giving me up. My mother said that is the greatest sacrifice a mother can make. And then she said that they actually got to pick me so I was loved by two mothers.

When I thought about it that way, I guess I thought I was pretty lucky. I've had a good life so

*far and two wonderful parents. Please know that
I don't blame you for your decision. You mentioned
having a lot of guilt at times and you don't need
to. I really am okay.*

*I have a sister named Tess who's two years
younger than me. She was adopted also so we
understand each other pretty well. Sometimes we
have emotions that others don't so we talk a lot.*

*After talking it over with my parents and Tess,
I decided I would like to meet with you. I'm starting college in about a month. Since I'll be away for
the next four years except for vacation, I thought
I should meet you in the next week. If that's okay,
that is.*

*You mentioned that your family wants to meet
me too. I think that would be too much for me the
first time but maybe we could plan something in
the future.*

Daniel

"Florence, that's wonderful. He sounds like a
fine young man," my mom said. The words kind of
cracked since she had started crying about halfway
through the letter.

"He does, doesn't he?" Aunt Florence hung onto
the letter.

215

I wiped my eyes. That phrase about him being okay really got to me. "Call him tonight," I said. "Otherwise, I won't get a chance to meet him for maybe four years."

Gramps and my dad were wiping their eyes too. They both cleared their throats.

"The boy is already going to college. It's hard to believe so much time has passed," Gramps said.

"I'm going to call him in a little while," Aunt Florence said.

"Florence, call him now," my mom said. "Go on."

"I have to wait until my heart slows down." She felt her pulse. "Okay, a couple of deep breaths and I should be fine." Aunt Florence took in two deep breaths. "Wish me luck."

"Good luck," I said.

"Good luck. Now go." My mom gently pushed Aunt Florence towards the basement.

She was back within fifteen minutes with the plans. She was meeting her son at a place called the St. Clair Broiler in St. Paul. It would be for lunch on Saturday and just the two of them. Aunt Florence said she didn't know how she was going to wait two more days. She had to work the next day and then tell them at work that she wouldn't be in on Saturday.

"Good for you, Florence. What did Mother used

to say? Bravo. Bravo, Florence." My mom hugged her sister.

"Hey, what about me?" I walked over for a group hug. Aunt Florence gave me a kiss on the cheek.

On Saturday, Aunt Florence changed her outfits three or four times. She finally settled on a gray pantsuit. She had a white blouse under it. My mom went upstairs and then came back with a red silk scarf. She tied it around her neck and stepped back. Two thumbs went up into the air.

"Florence, you look lovely. Just be yourself. Come here." Gramps hugged Aunt Florence. "I'm proud of you."

"Thank you. I better go." She put on her lipstick, brushed her hair, wiped her lipstick into a tissue, and straightened her scarf. She smoothed her suit jacket, pulled the sleeves down by her wrists, and checked the crease in her pants. She brushed her hair again and then gave it a quick squeeze. Out loud she said, "Okay."

"Good luck," I said. The problem was that I was going to have to wait all day to hear what my cousin, Daniel, was like and whether I was going to meet him before he went to college.

I hadn't been able to read anything all spring for the fun of it between Gramp's stroke and Mrs. Bosworth working us like dogs. Everything I had read had something to do with school. Not that I minded learning some things but it sure was nice to take a book outside, lay by a tree, and watch the clouds go by while listening to the birds. So that's what I decided to do. I grabbed a book from the pile in my room and proceeded to the back yard. I hoped the day would go by quickly so I didn't have to wait too long for Aunt Florence.

It was 10:00 pm before Aunt Florence returned to Red Wing. We all sat in the living room while she told us the story of meeting her son, Daniel at the St. Clair Broiler.

"I was a little early so I sat in a booth and waited," Aunt Florence said. "I saw Daniel through the window walking towards the front door. It was as though our brother, Daniel, was walking through the door. I would have recognized him anywhere. It was uncanny."

"Wow," my mom said.

"We were both nervous to begin with. I thought school would be a neutral subject so I asked him what he liked in school and what he was going to study in college."

"What was his answer?"

"He said he was thinking about Psychology but he really liked to write stories. So he's kind of nervous about college because he's not quite sure of what he wants to do."

Gramps had looked over at me when Aunt Florence said Psychology. He gave me a wink.

"Our brother liked to write too," my mom said.

"And you won't believe it, but Daniel loves the river. He puts the river in some of his stories," Aunt Florence said. "He did ask me about his father."

"What did you say?" my mom asked.

"I told him the truth. That I had loved Roy and didn't know he was married."

My dad leaned in towards Aunt Florence. "He wasn't fair to you, Florence," he said.

"I can't think about that. I put it behind me years ago," Aunt Florence said. "Anyway, Daniel asked me how old I was when I had him. I told him I was eighteen and that I had no way of taking care of him. Then he asked me if I was married now. I said I had never dated anyone but Roy."

"Did he reply to that?" my mom asked. She brought Aunt Florence a cup of hot coffee.

"Not right away. I had decided I would answer any question he asked me." Aunt Florence took a sip of her coffee. "Then he said, 'That must have been hard for you, Florence.' And I guess we both relaxed."

I felt kind of bad for all the times I had laughed and made fun of Aunt Florence never going on a date.

Aunt Florence continued. "I told him about all of you and my brother, Daniel. He told me about his family. And yes, Colette, he does play basketball."

"I knew it. I knew it," I said.

There wasn't a dry eye in the house when Aunt Florence told us Daniel thanked her for contacting the adoption agency. He said he was kind of mad at her for giving him up but he understood that it must have been an impossible situation. He said that her choice had allowed him to have two great parents. And he said he was glad they had met because she had answered his questions.

Aunt Florence said she thanked him for letting her spend so much time with him. She told him it was one of the most memorable days of her life. They shook hands for a long, long time when they said goodbye. Then he said he'd like to come to Red Wing to meet everyone. He said he'd have to check with his parents first because he was leaving in about three weeks. So they left it that he would call in the next week and hopefully set something up.

I don't think anybody noticed but my fingers had been crossed for the whole conversation. Now I uncrossed them and yelled, "Yes."

Chapter Twenty Five

Daniel

Two weeks later we waited in our house for my cousin, Daniel. My mom and Aunt Florence had been working on the meal all afternoon. My mom was in charge of the potato salad. I couldn't believe how much work it was. She was boiling potatoes, making hard boiled eggs, cutting and chopping up celery, onion, and radishes. I had wanted our famous rump roast but I was overruled since everybody was afraid it would be too hot to turn on the oven.

Aunt Florence had made a fresh peach pie for dessert. My dad said she was thinking about the old saying, "The way to a man's heart is through his stomach." He had bought corn on the cob since it was August and we were having hamburgers on the grill. He called it a perfect summer meal.

My dad took off work early so he could help too. The good china was out. My dad and I got the table ready with a lace tablecloth. Then we set the table with the good china and the good silverware.

Aunt Florence had told us that her son looked a lot like her brother, Daniel. Gramps grabbed his heart and said, "Oh, my God," under his breath when Daniel walked in our house.

"Nice to meet you, Daniel. Nice to meet you," Gramps said. He shook Daniel's hand.

"Nice to meet you too, Mr. Rossini."

"Call me Antonio."

They had started out very seriously but now both of them were grinning from ear to ear. Good old Gramps. How could you resist him?

When I was introduced, I said, "Do you like basketball?"

Daniel said, "Of course, how could you not?"

"That's exactly how I feel. Do you play?"

"I played in high school but I'm not going to in college. I'm not good enough."

"Can you do a jump shot?"

"Yeah, I can do a jump shot."

"I knew it."

"Colette will talk about basketball all night if you let her. Sit down," my mom said to Daniel. "Would you like something to drink?"

"Do you have a Coke?"

"Sure. I'll get you one."

"Me too, Mom," I said. I had to take advantage of the chance to have a Coke before dinner. I sat in the living room across from Daniel. "Just wait till you taste Aunt Florence's fresh peach pie. It almost melts in your mouth. I'd say it's out-of-this world."

"Is she a good cook?" Daniel asked.

I thought of what my dad had said. "The best," I said while sipping my Coke.

My dad and Gramps showed Daniel the garage. I wanted to go with them but my mom said she needed help. She said she would make the hamburger patties if I shucked the husks off of the corn. Aunt Florence had already started working on the corn. I decided I would pitch in without complaining or saying how unfair it was.

A big kettle waited on the stove for the corn. All you could hear was splash, splash as the corn was tossed into the kettle. With every splash I thought that's one less ear of corn I have to shuck.

My dad lit the coals in the grill when they were outside. He came in and said, "I'm just about ready. How are you doing?"

"The patties are ready," my mom said. She had the patties carefully stacked in layers with wax paper in between so they wouldn't stick to each other.

My dad grabbed the plate with the stacked burgers on it and headed out to the grill. He always stayed outside with his burgers. So we didn't see him again until they were done. We hurried when my dad yelled that the burgers were done. My mom took the corn out of the kettle and put it on a plate, Aunt Florence brought the potato salad to the table, and I carried the hamburger buns to the table in a basket.

We sat down. Gramps said, "Bless Us, Oh Lord," and "Thank you for my family," and we started passing the food around.

"Daniel, sometimes you have to yell for things at our dinner table," I said.

"I'll remember that."

"It's too bad we don't have crescent rolls because Aunt Florence could do one of her famous hook shots and sail it over to your plate."

"I'd like to see that," Daniel said.

"Okay. You asked for it." Aunt Florence took a hamburger bun out of the basket, pulled her arm back, and tossed the roll through the air in a perfect arc.

Daniel plucked the roll out of the air and put it on his plate. "I wouldn't want to play one-on-one with you," he said.

Aunt Florence giggled in her contagious way and so we all laughed. We couldn't help it. And there was so much conversation, I barely got a word in. But I didn't care. Not one little bit. We finished eating and just sat at the table, talking and laughing. All of a sudden, my mom remembered the pie.

"Daniel, how would you like your pie?" my mom asked. "Plain or a la mode?"

"A la mode, please."

"A boy after my own heart," Gramps said. "Load it up for me too."

Gramps exclaimed as usual about how great the pie was and the whole meal for that matter. I noticed Daniel holding his stomach so he must have been as stuffed as I was.

I couldn't believe my ears when my mom said, "Let's leave the dishes and go into the living room."

Gramps got out the photo albums. He showed Daniel pictures of Grandma Rose, her parents, Paddy and Marie, Mom and Aunt Florence growing up, my mom and dad's wedding, and me as a baby and little kid. And, of course, we all looked at the picture of Uncle Daniel in his uniform. Now, when I looked at my uncle and then looked at my cousin, the resemblance was incredible. The two Daniels could easily have been brothers. We were in a semi-circle around Daniel while he asked questions. He asked Gramps if he had any pictures from Ellis Island.

"No," Gramps said, "but I remember it like it was yesterday."

"I wish I would have known that because I would have interviewed you for my history paper last spring."

"Just let me know if it comes up again. I'll be happy to help."

I said, "I hope you've got a lot of time because Gramps loves to talk about Ellis Island."

"Maybe we can talk about it when I'm home for Christmas vacation," Daniel said.

"I'd like that," Gramps said. "I'd like that a lot."

Daniel told us at 9:00 pm that it was time for him to go. Gramps pumped Daniel's hand and then put his hand on his shoulder. "Good luck in school. I hope it goes well for you." He stood for a moment looking at Daniel. "Come here. No Italian grandfather would let his grandson leave without hugging him." He hugged Daniel and then kissed him on each cheek.

"Thank you for coming," my mom said. She gave him a quick kiss on the cheek.

"Thanks for inviting me," Daniel said.

"Don't mention it," my dad said. "You're welcome any time." He shook Daniel's hand. "You're family, you know."

"Bye, Daniel," I said. "I'm glad I have a cousin."

"Me too." He messed up my hair but I didn't care.

Aunt Florence and Daniel stood in front of the door, neither of them saying a word. It was Daniel who broke the silence.

"Florence, I really enjoyed this. Thank you."

"Thank you. You've made me very happy. Can I write to you?"

"I might not write back for a couple of weeks but I'd like that."

He turned to walk out the door and then turned around again to Aunt Florence. Neither of them said anything this time because they were too busy hugging. He walked out the door with all of us watching and yelling, "Good luck."

"Wait, Daniel. Can I write to you too?" I said.

Daniel turned around. "Sure, Colette. Write to me. I'd love to hear all about basketball season."

"Godspeed, Daniel," Gramps said.

"I'll call when I come back for Christmas," Daniel said before he closed his car door.

We all watched until the car taillights were out of sight.

"I can die happy now," Gramps said as he sat in his chair.

So that's my story. September is here. I'll be starting seventh grade in a couple of days and I won't have Mrs. Bosworth. Ta - Da! I won't ever have to watch "Becoming a Woman" again. Double Ta – Da!

Basketball season starts the first day of school. I'll be practicing one-on-one with Bobby Bennett every Saturday. Even though I told the Bloomer I was really going to miss her, I'm looking forward to playing without having to dive after one of her crazy passes. I'll have quite a cheering section this year since Aunt Florence said she isn't going to miss a game. I can hardly wait for our play-by-play discussions after each game.

I wonder if I'll look back on this summer of 1970 as the summer when my family really got to know each other. My mom said that we put old ghosts to rest. I've learned that sometimes people are just trying to spare each other's feelings. Like Gramps, for instance. He was trying to spare Aunt Florence and she was trying to spare him. So they never talked about either of the two Daniels. After all Aunt Florence's worry about how Gramps would react to meeting her son, Gramp's heart was on his sleeve. He actually said he could die happy.

I've decided I'm a pretty lucky girl. We have a brand-new garage that I helped build. Sally is the best

best-friend ever. I have the coolest dad in the world. I actually use my mom's sayings because they describe things so well. Aunt Florence is fun to be around these days. We're even thinking about driving up to St. Paul again so we can compare the fall colors along the banks of the river with Lake Pepin. And the best thing of all. I have a great cousin named Daniel who said I could write to him in college.

And Gramps. He told me he's making arrangements for us to go to Italy not next Summer but at Christmas. He said Chicago might have to wait a little longer. I'll keep my fingers crossed. All I can say about him is he's just Gramps. I wouldn't change anything about him. He's perfect just the way he is.

About the Author

Mary Clare is a retired Oncology/Hospice RN. She has a BA in Writing from Metropolitan State University. Her stories have appeared in Chicken Soup books, several magazines, and Handprints on My Heart on-line. She has self-published two books:  "Warning! Family Vacations May Be Hazardous to Your Health" and "Barefoot, Shoefoot." She has four daughters, three sons-in-law, and two and a half grandsons. She has been married to Paul for 35 years.